IN PURSUIT OF LOVE & CLOUT

KATHRYN REIGN

CONTENTS

IN Pursuit OF Love AND Clout

KATHRYN REIGN

CHAPTER 1

I wish it were summer. If it were summer, I could wear a flowy dress, and maybe some cute sandals. Show myself off a little. But since it's December, I have to tuck myself into a massive coat and a knitted hat. I consider leaving the hat at home. My hair always gets crazy staticky when I wear it, but it's far too cold.

Before I head out the door, I grab my phone and

read through our messages again, making sure I've got the time right.

And now I'm sweating again.

Not because of the coat. I'm sweating because of the fact that I'm about to go on a date with a *gorgeous* man who seems genuinely nice. Those are not easy to come by. Tanner and I matched on a dating app, and we've been texting nonstop for the past month. He finally asked me out on a date, and I guess I'm about to find out if I was being catfished all along, or if he's really that hot in real life.

Taking a look in the mirror, I see that I have a smudge of mascara in the corner of my eye. When I wipe it off, a black line drags across my cheekbone. Great.

While I clean it off my skin, I get a text.

Looking forward to seeing you.

It's from Tanner. I smile and start to type out a response, but I erase everything again. I let my fingers hover over the screen, and I bite my lip. I want to write something funny, something that'll make him think I'm hilarious. But also smart and sophisticated. My mind is blank. Maybe I'm none of those things, come to think of it. So instead, I say the most generic thing I can think of.

Me, too. About ready to leave.

Wow. That was probably the most boring text I've ever sent. I'll just have to dazzle him over coffee instead.

I slip my ankle boots on over my feet and give my

carefully curled hair one last look in the mirror before I drag my knitted hat over it. My heart is racing as I walk down the stairs, and the cold December air hits me as soon as I step outside. There are lights everywhere, and I can see some version of Santa Claus wherever I look. I haven't even gotten a tree yet, and I honestly don't think I will. I get enough of the holiday vomit just stepping out the door.

It's not a long walk to the coffee shop where we're meeting up, but I manage to slip on the icy sidewalk no less than three times before I get there. I feel *incredibly* graceful. The place is packed when I step inside, and I do a quick scan of the people sitting there. I can't see Tanner anywhere. I'm at the right place, aren't I?

Oh, crap. It's happening again. He's standing me up. I'm getting…

"Sophie?"

I turn around, and there he is. Tall, luscious hair that's styled to perfection, and a smile that lights up his face. God, he's cute. He's wearing a coat that looks warm without being bulky, like something you just throw on as a complementary piece to the rest of your outfit. There's a sprinkling of snow on his shoulders that look like dandruff, but that's the only sign that he didn't just step out from the pages of a fashion magazine. I then realize that I haven't said anything yet, so I force myself to smile.

"Hi!" I exclaim, a bit too loud. "It's great to finally meet you."

We do a sort of awkward half-hug thing, and he, of course, smells amazing. Deep and rich and *male*. I forgot to put on perfume today. Hopefully, my body wash does its thing.

"So," Tanner says, "coffee. What's your drink?"

I usually get some sort of frappé, or maybe a latte with extra foam. But maybe I should get something else. He looks like the type of guy who gets an espresso or just takes his coffee black.

"Um… I'll just have an espresso, I think."

"Yeah?" he asks, raising an eyebrow. "Are you sure?"

"Definitely. It's what I always get."

Tanner nods. "Okay, then. One espresso coming up." We walk up to the barista behind the counter. Tanner smiles at her, and I see her cheeks go pink. I can't blame the girl; he *is* positively swoon-worthy.

"Hi, there," he greets her. "One espresso for my friend here, please. And I'll have a latte. Extra foam."

Crap. I really want a latte, too. Instead, I'll have to make do with the tiny cup the barista hands me, filled with black tar. We find a table by one of the windows, and I finally get to take off my coat. It was getting a bit sweaty under there.

"There are so many people out today," Tanner remarks and looks outside.

"Well, it *is* December," I reply. "It's the busiest time of the year, especially in this town."

North Pole, Alaska. The Christmas Town. There's

always a lot of tourists around, but December is on a whole other level.

Tanner laughs. "Yeah, I was honestly a little shocked when I moved here. I never thought people could be *that* into Christmas."

"No? It's kind of right there in the name."

"I know," he responds with a smile. "But still. You grew up here, right? What's it like having Christmas all year round?"

"It's very… Christmas-y." I take a sip of the espresso. *Ugh.* "It's alright. I don't mind it, really. Some people up here get a little too excited, though."

"Yeah, I've seen some real enthusiasts around town. A lot of Santa hats."

"Why *did* you move here?" I ask. "We get a lot of tourists, but I don't really get why someone would actually come to live here. It's a pretty small town."

Tanner shrugs. "It's kind of a long story. Came here for love. Turned out, it was pretty one-sided."

"What do you mean?"

"I caught her fucking a guy from work."

I wince. "Ouch, that sucks. And you stayed here anyway?"

"I kind of like it here," he says, eyes fixed on me. "And with my job, I don't really have to worry about where I live. It's all remote, so…"

Right. Tanner's job. I've never met someone who can just support themselves with their social media presence. Must be nice parading around and taking pictures of yourself, *and* getting paid for it. He must be pretty popular, but I actually haven't checked him out online yet. Maybe that's a little weird; I'm just not on social media a lot.

"Must be exciting," I say. "Being able to work for yourself."

He nods. "It was never the plan, but I love it. I'm pretty lucky to get to do what I do." He leans forward, resting his arms on the table. "And you? Do you like what you do?"

"I work in a grocery store," I respond and roll my eyes. "Not exactly the most glamorous thing."

"Maybe not," Tanner says, and he looks at me with those amazing brown eyes that just make me melt. "But not everything has to be glamorous in order to be enjoyed."

You should like me just fine, then. "It's a pretty crappy job, to be honest. I'd rather do something else, but there aren't very many jobs available in this tiny town."

"You should start something on your own. Do something online; there are so many opportunities nowadays."

I nod. I have no idea what I would even do if I were to start my own business, but I don't want him to know that. "Maybe I'll just do what you're doing," I tease and smile.

"You should. It's very rewarding."

We sit there and talk for the better part of two hours. My espresso is long gone, and Tanner is actually laughing at my jokes. This is going better than I'd thought. I like the way he's so passionate about what he does. I'm not used to guys actually listening to what I have to say, but he seems genuinely interested in what I'm talking about, too. What kind of moron would cheat on a guy like this?

Tanner walks me back to my apartment, and our hands keep touching as we're strolling down the streets. When we stop outside my apartment building, he strokes my hair back from my face before he leans in close. A jolt of electricity shoots through me when our lips meet. His lips are soft, and when I open up for him, he tastes of coffee and mint. His tongue is teasing, and his fingers in my hair send shivers down my back.

"I hope to see you again soon," he says as we pull apart, his voice low and raspy. I nod and look into his eyes.

"I hope so, too."

I watch as he walks away, my skin tingling as if someone has opened a can of soda in my chest. That went way better than I thought it would.

I smile all the way up the stairs as I walk into my apartment. I can't sit still, so I just pace around my living room. Thinking back on the hours we spent at the coffee shop. I take out my phone, wanting to text him right away. But maybe that would be weird. Yeah, better to wait a little, at least until he gets home. I can be patient.

Who am I kidding? No, I can't.

Thanks for a lovely date. I look forward to seeing you again.

And then I send a little kissy face. Is that juvenile? I don't really care. I'm just so excited!

This feels like the start of something great.

CHAPTER 2

Tanner and I meet up a few more times that week. We go for walks around town, and he takes me out for dinner and drinks. And we kiss. He's such a good kisser. I used to think kissing was kind of boring. A nice little prelude to what's to follow, but with Tanner, I can spend ages kissing. I want to invite him up to my place, but I'm kind of nervous. I've been with my fair share of guys before, but none as great as him; none as gorgeous as him.

I call him every night before bed just to talk, and I send him a good morning text when I wake up. I can't help myself. I don't think I've ever felt so connected to another person as quickly as I have with Tanner.

Want to grab dinner tonight?

I send the text at work, even though I'm not supposed to have my phone on me. My boss never notices anyway, so I think I'm good. In between customers, I check to see if Tanner has answered. We haven't seen each other for a few days, and I can't wait to spend time with him again. Right before my shift's over, my phone dings.

Sure, come over. I'll cook for you.

My stomach does a little flip as I read through the words again. I haven't been to Tanner's place yet; we've mostly seen each other at different places around town. This is a good sign, isn't it? Him inviting me over? I spend ages getting ready, curling my hair and choosing my outfit carefully. Tanner's clothes always seem so effortlessly put together; I don't understand how he does it.

I eventually settle on some jeans and a light blue top with cut-out shoulders. Casual but pretty enough. Tanner's apartment building is one of the new ones downtown, and when I take the elevator up to the fourth floor, I can't help but notice the differences from where I live.

My place is decent; I shouldn't complain. But this is so nice! Fresh and modern and probably really expensive. Tanner can obviously afford it, though. We haven't discussed things like that, but people in his line of work make plenty of money, don't they? Not that it matters; I'd like him regardless.

I find his apartment quickly and knock on the door. Tanner greets me with a hug and a warm smile, with a glass of wine in one hand.

"Come in! I just finished dinner," he says and offers me a glass of wine, too. "I hope you like salmon."

"I love salmon!" I exclaim, sipping my wine. I look around the large living room on our way to the kitchen. Tanner's apartment has massive windows and dark hardwood floors that seem to surround the place. A big Christmas tree takes up a corner of the living room, beautifully decorated in red and gold.

"This place is gorgeous," I whisper, and Tanner smiles.

"Thanks, I got lucky when I got it. There weren't many places for sale when I moved into town."

We go into the kitchen, and it smells amazing. Tanner finishes setting the table, and there are even lit candles.

"Wow, you really went all out."

"I don't have company over very often," he says and pulls out a chair for me. "I guess I wanted to make a good impression."

"Well, you've absolutely done that," I reply and sit down.

Tanner plates some salmon and pasta for me, and

I help myself to the salad. He sits down opposite me and raises his glass.

"I'm glad you came tonight," he says as our glasses clink together. "I've enjoyed spending time with you lately."

I try to school my face into a cool expression, but I can't quite hold back the massive grin that springs forth at his words. "Me, too. I've enjoyed it a lot."

"I'm glad." He pauses, some of the warmth leaving his eyes. "I've had a bit of a hard time letting someone in after what happened with my ex."

"I get it." I take a bite of the fish. The salmon is practically falling apart as I bite into it. I almost moan when all the flavors hit me at once.

"I want to put all that behind me, though."

I smile. "I hope you can do that with me."

"I hope so, too." Tanner reaches across the table and takes my hand. "I just need us to take things slow. I hope that's okay."

"Of course," I answer him, but there's a hint of disappointment that settles in my stomach. "Whatever you need."

"Oh, good!" He looks relieved. Has he been stressing over this that much? "I was afraid you wouldn't be on the same page about this."

"No, I want you to be comfortable," I tell him, even though he's kind of right. "We'll take things as they go. No pressure."

"Thank you." He brings my hand up to his lips and presses a soft kiss to my knuckles. "More wine?"

"Please." I hand him my glass and watch him fill it up again. I shouldn't feel bad. It's not like he said we should stop seeing each other or anything. But I'm not a "take it slow" kind of girl. I'm all in. I thought Tanner was, too. We've been talking every day since we first met, for Heaven's sake. Doesn't that mean anything?

I shouldn't overthink it, though. It's not a big deal if he wants to take it slow.

It isn't.

I manage to put our conversation out of my mind and just enjoy the evening. After dinner, he brings out a massive carton of ice cream, and we eat right out of the tub on the couch, with a movie on in the background. I can barely follow the plot; I keep glancing over at Tanner. He has one arm around my shoulders, and the warmth from his body is making me kind of drowsy. I could get used to this. Us two, just having a quiet evening together on the couch. Talking and laughing together. How am I supposed to take this slow?

I yawn and nuzzle closer to his side. Tanner smiles down at me and kisses me on my temple.

"Are you getting tired?"

"A little," I tell him.

"Maybe we should call it a night, then? It *is* getting late."

I smile up at him. "I could stay over."

Tanner's smile gets a little stiffer than before. "Sophie, I…"

"Sorry," I interrupt. "We're taking things slow, I know." I try to sound light and breezy when I talk, like it's no big deal, but my embarassment is shining through as my cheeks turn red. I get out from under his arm and stand up. "No worries. I'll just see you some other time."

Tanner gets on his feet, leaning in for a kiss. I sink into him, loving the way he caresses my cheek. "Thanks for understanding," he says as we pull apart. "I just don't want us to rush into things before we're ready."

I'm ready, I want to say. *I'm so fucking ready.* But I just nod. "No, I get it. It's a good thing, really. Gives us a chance to get to know each other."

"Exactly!" he practically yells, making me feel even worse. "I think so, too."

Great. Awesome. I force myself to keep smiling as I head for the door. I smile through our goodbye kiss, and I smile as I head downstairs. When I hit the street, I let my face fall. Why does this feel so bad? He likes me; he said so! And I get that his ex kind of messed him up a little. I get why he wants to be a little cautious. It's just going to be hard. I want to see him all the time. Talk to him all the time.

I take a deep breath. It's okay.

I'm okay.

CHAPTER 3

We continue to see each other every now and then, but Tanner has an influencer event coming up, and less and less time to see me. I try not to let it hurt my feelings, but it does. It feels like he's avoiding me. I call him every day, though, needing to hear his voice. The phone calls are short; he keeps saying how busy he is, but I take what I can get.

Another week passes, and the time has come for

him to go to his event. I don't really understand what someone does at an event for influencers, but I guess it's a big deal. Tanner seems excited, at least, so I try to seem excited as well. He's only going to be gone for three days, but I already know I'm gonna miss him like crazy.

"Call me when you get there, okay?" I ask him.

Tanner smiles at me. "I'll send you a text, Sophie," he says and loads his designer suitcase into his car. "I'll be busy, so don't freak out if you don't hear from me right away."

"No, no, I won't," I spit out quickly, even though I know I probably will freak out a little. Or a lot.

"Good. I'll see you in a few days, okay?"

He pulls me in for a quick peck, but I hold onto the lapels of his jacket, deepening the kiss. He smiles and winks at me.

"See you soon."

"Can't wait," I respond and wave goodbye, standing there on the curb as he drives off. There's a lump in the pit of my stomach all of a sudden. I know we've only known each other for a few weeks, but I like Tanner.

I like him a lot.

I take out my phone, typing out a text.

Drive safe.

There's no answer. But he's driving, so I don't really worry about it. Instead, I head back to my place, glancing at my phone every couple of minutes just in case he writes me back. At the apartment, I plop down onto my couch, throwing some random sitcom on in the background, my pomeranian jumping up beside me and snuggling against my chest. I hardly notice what's going on; my mind is elsewhere.

Why hasn't he texted me back? How hard is it to just type out a short text? I put my phone on the coffee table with the screen down so I won't think about it, but I grab it only seconds later. No message. I type out a text and send it to him.

I hope there's not too much traffic. I hate driving when there's a lot of traffic.

Send.

I frown at my screen. What the hell was that? Did I really just send him a text about traffic? He must think I'm so annoying, but I can't help it. I feel like I have to keep texting him, keep in contact somehow. I feel like I can't relax otherwise.

After about two hours, I finally get a text back from Tanner. By that time, I'd already sent him three more.

Everything is good. I'm just taking a break. Grabbing lunch now. Is everything good back in Santa Town?

I smile. He's been calling the North Pole "Santa Town" for a while now, with good reason.

Everything's good here. I'm about to head to work.

No answer. It's no big deal, I tell myself. He's at a work event. It's fine. I go and change into my uniform, popping on that infernal Santa hat that we have to wear the entire month of December. I don't bother putting on any makeup; I just don't feel like it.

As I head downstairs, I check my phone again. Nothing. *He's working,* I think to myself. *Don't overthink this.*

The drive to the grocery store only takes ten minutes, and as soon as I walk through the doors, my boss scuttles up to me.

"Sophie, you're late," he sternly says to me, pointing to the massive wristband he's always wearing. I frown, looking at the time on my phone.

"I start at eleven."

"Well, you're two minutes late," Eric, my boss, says, shaking his head in disapproval. "You know, punctuality is something we value here at the company. After all these years, I would have thought you knew that. I'm afraid I'm going to have to write you up."

Asshole. "Okay, fine," I mutter, resisting the urge to roll my eyes. Eric is a tiny man who inherited this store from his mother. I don't think I've ever seen him do any actual work. He just runs around making sure all his little elves don't slack off. Not exactly a relaxing work environment.

"I'll have you know that a lot of people would treat their job here with respect," he continues. "A lot of young girls would be happy to fill your role."

Ugh. I hate it when he calls me a *young girl.* I'm twenty-six, for fuck's sake. And he must've bonked his head on something hard if he thinks people are lining up to work at his little shitty grocery store. Last year when someone quit, he couldn't fill the role for nearly four months. It was kind of funny, actually. I know my job is safe.

"Am I on the cash register today?" I ask, and he nods.

"Yes, and go tell Lacey to head out back. We have a delivery coming in any minute now."

He turns around to leave, and I head over to the registers. Lacey is sitting there, just staring into space. She's chewing a piece of gum, as always, popping it with the most bored expression I think I've ever seen. There are no customers at the moment, as is usually the case, and when she sees me, her face brightens.

"Are you here to relieve me from this hell?" she asks.

I nod. "Yeah, you're needed out back. There's a delivery."

"Thank, God!" she exclaims, stepping out from behind the conveyor belt. "This has been the slowest morning ever!"

As if it's ever busy at the store. Most people tend to shop at the bigger supermarket right outside of town. There's way more there, with much cheaper prices. Even I do that, and I work here!

As I predicted, it continues to be a slow day. Things start to pick up a little in the afternoon, but I still have time to check my phone every now and then. Tanner still hasn't texted me back. I hide my phone when my boss walks by, a sour look on his face, but I take it out again as soon as he's gone.

I go to one of Tanner's social media profiles. He's posted a couple of pictures, including one where he's standing in front of a massive brick wall, riddled with street art. He's smiling, shielding his eyes from the sun with his hand, and he's wearing an outfit that I haven't seen before. A pair of dark blue jeans and a chunky knitted sweater that would look ridiculous on anyone else.

Somehow, he manages to make it look good, though. He'd look good in anything, his tall and slim physique the perfect body type for even the most hideous of clothes. I guess that's why he has so many followers. I keep scrolling and see another picture of him with a woman in a tight, blue dress. They're both looking into the camera with sultry eyes, and there's a hint of a smile on Tanner's lips.

I sigh. Damn, he's cute. The woman is gorgeous, and I see that he's tagged her in his caption. Brandy Daiko. I have no idea who she is, but when I click on her profile, I see that she has millions of followers. Her feed is just pictures of herself, wearing one extravagant outfit after another.

How do she and Tanner know each other? I guess through work, but I want to know how *well* they know each other. I scour her profile to see if he shows up in any of her pictures, but I don't find anything. For some reason, that makes me feel better. Only a little, however. She really is gorgeous. The type of beauty that doesn't seem real. There are probably a lot of girls like her in his line of work. Beautiful, confident, adored by everyone around them.

Girls like Brandy probably get more attention from guys than she knows what to do with. I can't even imagine what her DMs must look like. It shouldn't make me feel so insecure just seeing her standing next to the guy I'm dating. I know Tanner likes me, but there's still a nagging feeling in the pit of my stomach that won't go away.

I turn on my camera and snap a picture slightly from above. I send it to Tanner and add the words: *Having the time of my life here. I hope your day is going better than mine.*

To my surprise, Tanner actually answers right away.

Are you Santa's Little Helper today?

Yeah, if Santa were the biggest asshole on the planet.

Rough day, huh?

It's alright. My boss is just kind of a jerk. How are things over there?

It's good. I've been to a few workshops that have been really interesting. There are some new features on one of the platforms I'm on that sounds really cool. I have a couple of meetings this afternoon, so I might not be able to get to my phone.

I'm not sure what to say about the cool new features he's talking about, so I just send him a smiling face. I really want to ask him if we can talk later. I want to hear his voice. Maybe that's too much, though. He *did* say that he's going to be busy. I'm just going to have to be patient.

WHEN MY SHIFT is finally over, I hurry back home. Despite knowing that he can't talk, I really want to talk to Tanner. *Need* to talk to him. I dial his number, listening as the signals go through. I get to his voice-mail, but I don't leave a message. I'll just have to try again later.

I grab a frozen dinner from my freezer and pop it into the microwave, and then I try calling him again. No answer. This time, a text comes through.

Sophie, I told you I'd be busy tonight. I'll talk to you tomorrow.

My heart picks up speed. Is he annoyed with me? Crap! I put away my phone, resisting the urge to call again just to explain myself. I can hold out until tomorrow, can't I? Instead of giving into temptation, I head off to bed.

I scroll through Tanner's feed again as I lie there. There's a new post with a picture of some people up on a stage. One of the workshops he was talking about, I guess. Tanner's caption mentions something about sustainability and their responsibility as influ-encers, but I don't really read through the whole thing. I keep scrolling, marveling at the number of likes and comments he gets on each and every post.

I can't even begin to comprehend having

hundreds of thousands of people following me. Having so many people know about my life. It seems kind of weird. Scary, even. And maybe a bit exhilarating. I open up my own profile. I almost never post on there, but maybe it might be fun if it's something I would take more seriously.

Tanner's photos are always so professional, and with all the engagement he's getting, it must be kind of fun. I glance up at the number of followers on my profile. Thirty-seven. I bet he gets that many new followers every thirty-seven minutes. I snap a picture of myself, still wearing that goddamn Santa hat for some reason.

This elf is exhausted. Are there unions for Santa's helpers?

I post it, not sure if it's cute or cringe-worthy. I get some likes from family and friends, but that's about it. How do I even begin to try and reach new people? And why would they follow me? I'd need better photos to start. Maybe I should try and up my social media game while Tanner is away. As a distraction, if nothing else. Can't hurt to try.

It's too dark to get any good pictures, but I'm too excited not to give it a go. I light some candles, and I find a string of fairy lights that I put up over the couch behind me. Grabbing a cute mug, I sit down and press the timer on my camera. I look off to the side, my legs tucked up under me. I hear the camera go off, and I hurry over to see the result. Not bad, actually. I'll just have to mess with the color setting a little, and then it should be good to go!

Tanner's right; this is fun! I continue with my little photo shoot for hours, trying on different outfits and settings. It feels good to be creative. I don't even remember the last time I actually created something.

Maybe I should give this whole thing a go?

CHAPTER 4

I call Tanner the following two nights as well, and we talk for a few minutes. If I'm being honest, it kind of sounds like he's a bit annoyed with me. On the day he's supposed to drive back home, he doesn't pick up the phone at all. I try to keep busy, snapping a few new shots for my profile. I've actually gained a few followers; I'm up to forty-three now!

Every time I get a notification, my heart starts

beating a bit faster. It's just so exciting seeing the likes tick up. I decide to take some pictures outside while wearing a new dress that I just bought the other day, and I pose in front of one of the massive Santas that are peppered around town with my little pomeranian. It turns out really cute, and I post it after messing with the colors and lighting for a few minutes. There's instantly a like from a profile I don't recognize.

DonnieWylde93. His profile picture shows a guy with a buzz cut, his chin raised, and his light eyes looking at the camera with lowered lids. He kind of looks like a fuck boy, but who am I to judge? I do notice that he has almost ten thousand followers, although I'm not sure why. What's his secret? He only seems to put up shirtless pictures of himself. I look through his profile, and a couple of seconds later, I see that DonnieWylde93 is following me and has left a comment under my post.

Damn, you're hot.

I know I should be at least a little bit outraged by his words, by the possessive, objectifying way he writes. But I feel a small thrill inside. Does that make me a bad feminist? Probably. In any case, I don't respond to Donnie, but those words echo in my head for the next hour. I'm not used to being told that I'm hot. Maybe I am? My thoughts are interrupted when a text from Tanner lights up my screen.

Can I swing by your place when I get back into town? I'll be there in about twenty minutes.

He's almost back already? That was quick; he

probably didn't take very many breaks along the way. I smile and practically run back home to straighten up the place. Lucky for me, I'm still wearing my new dress. I hope Tanner will appreciate it as much as DonnieWylde93 did.

My doorbell rings exactly twenty minutes later, and I fluff up my hair in the mirror before I answer the door. Tanner looks kind of tired, and he only half hugs me back when I fling my arms around him.

"I'm so glad you're back!" I yell joyfully, holding onto his arm.

"Yeah, um…" He looks a bit nervous, not really meeting my eyes. "Can we talk for a second?"

"Of course!" I cheer again. "Want some coffee or something?"

Tanner shakes his head, dragging a hand through his hair. "No, thank you. I can't stay."

Disappointment settles in my stomach. "Oh, okay. So, what do you want to talk about?"

"Let's sit down," he says, dragging me to the couch. I see him swallow, and it's like he's bracing himself for something. Then he opens his mouth. "Sophie, I really like you."

"I really like you, too," I say back, trying to keep the smile on my face. Something in his tone worries me.

"It's just that, over the past few days, you've kind of been coming on a little strong."

Shit. "Well, I'm sorry if I'm a little enthusiastic," I try to explain, an edge to my voice. "I don't play games, Tanner. If I like someone, I'm going to show it."

"And that's great," he assures me. "But I've told you several times that I was busy, and you just kept calling and texting. We're not a couple, Sophie. We've only been seeing each other for a few weeks. I've already told you that I want to take things slow. I would like to keep seeing you, but I don't know if that's such a good idea if we're in different places all the time."

"I don't understand," I whisper quietly. "You want to keep seeing me, but not if I show you how much I like you?"

"You're twisting my words," he says with a sigh. "I don't mean that you can't contact me or anything. I like that you like me. It's just a bit much too soon."

"So, what are you saying?" I ask, swallowing a lump in my throat. "You don't want to see me anymore?"

"I think it's best if we just put on the brakes a little bit," Tanner replies softly, and he takes my hand. I yank it free, placing my hands on my lap.

"Fine," I answer with a pout. "If that's what you want."

"Sophie, I'm sorry if I've hurt your feelings. I just don't think we want the same things right now."

"Got it." My words are coming out short and curt. "You can leave now."

Tanner stands up and looks at me like he has more to say. He opens his mouth, but then changes his mind. He walks over to the door, and right before he leaves, he turns around and looks at me.

"I really am sorry."

"You said that already. Bye!"

He sighs again, but he doesn't say anything else. He just closes the door behind him and walks away. I sit frozen in place on the couch. He thinks I'm coming on too strong? Sure, maybe I called one time too many, but why should I hold back? I'm not one to play hard to get; I wear my feelings on my sleeve. Is that really so bad?

Damn it! I wipe at my eyes, tears falling down my cheeks. I don't want to cry over him. He's just some guy, and we didn't really know each other all that well. But the way he smiled at me, the way he held me and kissed me… It felt real. Special. But I guess it was just me who thought so.

I go to his profile and check it for the hundredth time that day. I scroll to the photo of him and Brandy Daiko.

Wait a minute. Did something happen between them during this trip? They look awfully cozy in the picture, that's for damn sure. Maybe this was just a convenient excuse to end things with me. I slam the phone against the couch and let out a groan. I bury my face in my hands, rubbing at my eyes.

Maybe Tanner is one of those guys who need their girlfriend to be someone. Maybe he needs someone with a following of her own. Someone he can use on his own socials. I pick up my phone again and open my own profile. Fifty-six followers now, and I have a DM from DonnieWylde93. A picture of him shirtless, biting his bottom lip. *Fuck boy*.

I go back to my profile and scroll through my images. I could be that person. I could create the same thing that Tanner has. A brand, a big following. That would certainly get his attention. I can do that, right? How hard can it be? I've already gained some followers over the past few days when I've posted my pictures. I just need to crank it up a notch. I need some new clothes. Something a bit more out there than my usual wardrobe; something that would look good when people scroll through their feed.

Maybe I should get a camera, too, a proper one. My phone works alright, but if I bought a professional camera, my pictures would probably perform even better. I search online and read reviews for different equipment and wince. *Damn, that's expensive.* I have some savings, but not a lot. I don't get paid a lot down at the grocery store, but I do have a few thousand stored away. That money is supposed to be stowed away for a rainy day, but it certainly feels like that day has come. Worst case scenario, I can just sell some old jewelry if I really need to.

I buy one of the cameras that has the best reviews, and as I put in my information, I get a mix of dread and exhilaration throughout my body. I really shouldn't spend so much, but it's an investment. Who knows? Maybe this social media thing takes off. Then I'll be glad to have invested in my future.

I look up one of the fashion brands that I know Tanner has worked with in the past, and I check out their website. Their clothing is a bit more risqué than I'm used to, but I still buy a couple of dresses and a flimsy little top that hardly looks like it'll hold my breasts in place. Whatever, I'll just have to make it work.

I wonder what Tanner would think if I got more followers than him. I know it's probably a long shot. But then again, why shouldn't I be able to get more followers than him? It's possible. I decide then and there to do it. I'm going to beat Tanner at his own game.

I look up how to gain more followers and read through pretty generic tips and tricks. I purse my lips. It seems like it will probably take quite a while to get to Tanner's level. I want to do this *now*. I search for *how to gain followers fast*, and I get more of the same type of bullshit advice. Post regularly, make sure to engage with your audience. Things like that. But then I see something that catches my eye.

Thousands of followers guaranteed. High quality.

I click on the link. Huh. It's a website that sells followers. I didn't even know that was a thing! The website looks a bit shady, and the information is pretty vague on how it works. It's kind of pricey, but I stay there anyway and read through the different options several times. It *does* seem a bit disingenuous, but it would be a means to an end. My goal is to get more followers than

Tanner, and this is most likely the quickest way to achieve that.

Should I do it? Maybe just to get the ball rolling. I add the option to gain a thousand followers to the cart and go and grab my card. I hesitate for a second, but then I imagine the look on Tanner's face when he sees what I have accomplished. I'll do the other stuff later, the consistency and engaging with the people who follow me. This is just to get started.

Proceed to checkout.

CHAPTER 5

It's like someone has waved a magic wand.

When I wake up the next day, I have a thousand new followers. They all have a profile picture and some posts on their feed as far as I can tell, which makes me feel better somehow. Like they're actual people. I know most of them probably aren't, but it at least looks like they are. Some even liked and commented on my most recent post! Pretty generic stuff, but still!

Excitement rushes through me, and I keep checking my profile as I get ready for work. I'm working the early shift today, so things should be pretty slow. I put on makeup, more than I usually would, and I fix my hair into loose curls. It takes forever, but it's worth it. I take a picture of myself in front of the window to get the best lighting, and then I post it. Some likes instantly come in, and I go to each of the profiles. Most are the bots I bought, but there seem to be actual people as well. Among them is DonnieWylde93. Only moments later, he sends me another DM.

Did you like the picture I sent you, sweetheart?

Sweetheart? Ugh. I scroll up to the shirtless pic he sent a few days ago. I mean, he looks good. If he'd just drop the douchebag expression on his face, he might even be handsome. I don't know why I answer him, but I do.

No, but you obviously love it. That's all that matters; believe in yourself!

Three little dots appear almost instantly, indicating that he's typing back. *Got a bit of a mouth on you, huh? I like that. Send me a pic.*

There are pics on my profile.

You know what I mean. A pic just for me.

The message is followed by a winky face and a peach emoji. Is he asking for nudes? Hell no! He's got some nerve asking that of me. *Not happening, dude. Gotta go.*

Guess I'll have to make do with what you've already posted. You know, you'd get so many more views if you showed off that body of yours. I bet it's really hot. I could promote it on my page. My followers are really into that sort of thing.

I look down at my chest. I *do* have pretty good breasts. Maybe it wouldn't be the worst thing in the world to show them off a little. Not like porn, but maybe some low-cut tops or something like that. Because Donnie is right. I'd get a hell of a lot more eyes on me if the pictures are of something other than my face. People do it all the time on social media, don't they? And if he'd be willing to give me a shout-out or something, then it would just work out in my favor.

The idea is actually a little exhilarating. I decide to give it a shot, but first, I need to get to work. Eric won't be happy if I show up late again.

My mind is barely present as I stock the shelves at work. Every chance I get, I check my profile. I've gained some more followers, not a lot, but at least it's something. Maybe the bots pushed my profile higher in the algorithm or something. Should I buy another thousand maybe? It obviously boosted some organic traffic to my profile. I'll think about it.

WHEN MY SHIFT is finally over, I head downtown to get something to drink at the coffee shop where

Tanner and I had our first date. It kind of hurts when I walk in through the door, but I push those feelings away. He dumped me, and I'm just going to have to get over it.

I order a latte to go and head back outside. I want to take a cute picture of the coffee, and I walk around for almost twenty minutes trying to find the perfect spot. The coffee is almost gone by the time I simply decide to put the cup in the snow, and I toss my mittens beside it. I arrange it so it looks nice and take my shot.

Some coffee to warm me up.

I post and toss the empty cup in a nearby trash can. Donnie has left a comment on the picture, and I roll my eyes as I read it.

You don't need coffee for that. I can come over and warm you up, sweetheart. Have you thought about what I said before?

Well, he's got confidence, at least. I have to give him that. I type out a response.

I'll send you a picture later. But only if you make good on your word about promoting my page.

Of course, sweetheart. My followers are going to love you.

I wonder if he's just saying that. Well, it can't hurt to give it a go. If Donnie can get me some new followers, then it's all good.

It's getting kind of cold, so I decide to go back home. Halfway back to my apartment building, it starts snowing again, and it's getting darker by the minute. Two packages are waiting for me outside my door, and I carry them inside with a big smile on my face. Must be the camera I ordered and my new clothes.

I try on every piece as soon as I walk through the door, and I pose in front of my mirror. I look pretty sexy, if I do say so myself. There's one dress, in particular, that does *great* things to my body. It hugs my curves in an amazing way, and the muted pink color is a pretty contrast to the low-cut neckline. Innocent and suggestive all at once. I love it! It would be perfect for the picture I'm going to send to Donnie.

Taking my new camera, I set it up on my kitchen table. It would probably be a good idea to get a tripod, but in the meantime, this will do. I try out a few different poses, trying to show off my new dress. I lean forward close to the camera and smile wide as the timer goes off. *Bingo.* I look happy and sweet, but my chest is very clearly the focal point of the picture. Not too much, but it's still sexy.

I chuckle to myself. I hope this will be good enough to bring in some people once Donnie posts it to his feed. I edit the image on my computer, then I send it to him. Donnie answers right away.

You trying to kill me, sweetheart?

I smile, shaking my head at him. I know he's just some random guy, but it's kind of nice to know that someone finds me attractive.

Are you uploading it or what?

Posting it now.

I keep a close eye on his profile, and after a few minutes, I see my picture pop up on there. The post gets almost three hundred likes within the first ten minutes, and I can't hold back a smile. Actual people are liking my picture! Sure, it's all guys, but that doesn't matter. It gets a few comments.

So hot.

Do one without the dress.

Stuff like that. Maybe not the type of followers I had originally envisioned, but I'll take it! It doesn't really matter who follows me, as long as it's a lot of people.

After my follower count slowly starts to trickle up, I go and check Tanner's profile. I just can't help myself. He posted a picture of him in front of a house that's decked out in Christmas decorations. I know the place; there's a street right outside of downtown that goes crazy in December. Their electricity bill must be through the roof!

Tanner is smiling, dressed in a nice coat and a knitted beanie. The caption says: *North Pole, Alaska is really living up to its name.*

There are thousands of likes and hundreds of comments. I bite my bottom lip, my excitement from before gone. He's still so far ahead of me. It's going to take ages to get to his numbers, even if I get other people to promote me.

I glance over at my computer. What can a thousand more bots hurt? I pull out my card before I can change my mind, and then there they are. Another thousand added to my follower count. That's going to have to be enough for a while. I've already spent hundreds of dollars over the past couple of days. It'll be worth it, though.

It will.

CHAPTER 6

My second boost of bots has made my images appear to other users as well. I get new followers daily, although not *that* many. It's fun seeing the numbers tick up, and I really enjoy the comments that I'm getting.

Maybe it's a little pathetic to lap up what these guys are saying to me, but I'm kind of loving the way they seem to be drooling over my pictures. It's sort of intoxicating. And DonnieWylde93 is always there as soon as I upload a picture. I know I probably shouldn't enjoy the attention from him as much as I am, but I can't help myself. It's kind of hot knowing that my pictures make him so excited.

He sent me more pictures of himself shirtless, but he never goes further than that. I've messaged him a bit back and forth, and it's clear that he wants things to escalate further. From what I understand, he doesn't live that far away; maybe an hour away.

Sometimes, I imagine myself meeting up with him, just to see what would happen. I'm honestly not all that attracted to him, and he's kind of an ass, but there's also something intriguing about that. One night of meaningless sex with someone so self-confident would be kind of fun. And he has already proven to be useful to me when he uploaded my picture.

Donnie would *definitely* drive all the way over here if I told him that the two of us getting together is on the table. Not that it *is* on the table; at least, I don't think so. But when he messages me late one night just as I'm about to go to bed, I can't help but write back.

I like your shirt in your last post.

I hesitate, but then I type out a reply. *Thanks, it's new.*

Donnie responds at once. *Are you wearing it right now?*

I look down at myself. I'm wearing an old sweater and some shorts to bed, not exactly a sexy négligée. *No, I'm not.*

What are you wearing?

Am I going there? Am I really going to start sexting with this fuck boy? I kind of want to. *It's too hot in here to wear anything.*

Oh, crap, I did it! My heart is racing as I see him writing something. I've never sexted before in my life, so maybe it's about time I get to experience it. My screen lights up with Donnie's message.

That's really hot, sweetheart. How come you're not sleeping?

I huff out a laugh; it's so obvious what he wants me to say. So, I say it. *I don't know. I guess I've been a little stressed lately. I just need something to take the edge off.*

You should make yourself feel good. Would you like that?

I clench my thighs together. I actually *am* getting a bit excited. *Yes.*

Donnie sends another picture, but this time, it's not his upper body I'm looking at. A massive bulge is straining against his underwear. *See what you do to me, sweetheart?*

I bite my lip. I won't send him any pictures. I have to draw the line somewhere, but I keep writing. *Careful, you'll poke someone's eye out with that thing.*

His reply comes at once. *Touch yourself for me, sweetheart. I want you to cum for me.*

I squirm under the covers. Slowly, I reach a hand under the waistband of my shorts. *How should I do it?* I ask him.

Just touch yourself for me. Pretend I'm right there in bed with you. Making you feel good.

I do as he says. Well, it's not exactly Donnie that

I'm imagining as I touch myself. Tanner's gorgeous face is the only thing I can think about. My breathing deepens, and I moan as I hit a perfect rhythm.

Sweetheart, are you still there?

Right. Donnie. *What else would you do to me if you were here?*

I'd make you moan and scream out my name.

I don't think I'd scream out his name. Donnie isn't exactly the sexiest name out there. But the thought of wrapping my legs around a hard body makes me pick up my pace. I haven't had sex in so long, and in that moment, I'd take just about anyone. Even Donnie.

I wonder what it would be like if Tanner were here, though. What it would be like to have him touching me like this. Oh, I'm getting close. Would he be rough, or is he more the love-making type? I bet he's amazing in bed, just like he is with everything else. If kissing him was any indication, then he must be *good*.

I cry out as my release starts to build, imagining what it would be like if I wasn't alone in bed. It's so good that I've forgotten all about my little sexting session with Donnie. Stars flash before my eyes as I bring myself over the edge. As my breathing slows, I see three new messages from Donnie.

Are you there?

Did you fall asleep, sweetheart?

Are you close? I'm so close right now, thinking of you.

I consider not answering him, but I shoot him a final message anyway. *That was pretty hot.*

It actually was. Donnie doesn't need to know that I imagined another man, though. Let him think I came, crying out *his* name. I pull the covers up to my chin, blissfully tired. I have work first thing tomorrow, but after that, I want to take some more pictures.

I ordered a new pair of heels that my followers are going to love, and I want to take some photos while wearing them. Maybe I'll get up extra early so I can post as soon as I can.

I reach for my phone, setting my alarm. I fall asleep despite the buzzing excitement that rushes through my body. It feels good to be creating something.

CHAPTER 7

I'm stocking the shelves at work when I take a short break to check my phone. I go to Tanner's profile. It's pretty much part of my daily routine by this point. I frown when I see that he has gained almost twenty thousand new followers since the last time I looked at it. Twenty thousand? That's insane! I bite my lip, thinking. I have already spent a lot on the bots, but I need to crank things up a notch if this is going to work. Otherwise, it will all have been for nothing.

Maybe I can ask Mom for a loan. I wouldn't tell her what it's for, obviously, just that I'm low on funds at the moment. Which is true. But just the idea of going to my mother for money makes me sick to my stomach. We aren't exactly close, and I've made the mistake of borrowing money from her in the past. I'll never hear the end of it.

I do get paid by the end of the week. If I just cut out any unnecessary spending, I can buy a bigger batch of bots. Maybe a few thousand this time.

I'll do that as soon as my shift is over.

"Are you on your phone, Sophie?"

I whirl around, like a deer in headlights, and see my boss staring at me, scowling with his hands on his hips. I slide my phone into my pocket.

"Sorry, Eric. It was an emergency."

Now he's crossing his arms over his chest. "An emergency? What kind of emergency?"

"It's…," I try to think frantically, "personal. Won't happen again, promise."

"I sure hope not," he says, obviously not believing me. "And you should be done with this shelf by now. There's a lot more that needs to be put on the shelves before your shift is over. You don't want to stay late, do you?"

"No, I'll hurry," I quickly answer, and he finally leaves me alone.

As soon as Eric is out of sight, I take out my

phone again. I look for the price to up my follower count with five thousand bots, and my stomach does a little flip. *Crap.* But then I remember Tanner's twenty thousand new followers. I have to do it. I just have to!

I ALMOST CRY when I look at my bank account balance after buying more followers that evening. It's for the best, I tell myself. And it's not like I'm not getting new followers that are actual people, too. I watch my notification like a hawk, and when I see a name I recognize, I almost jump out of my chair.

Patrick Amaranth has followed me. I have to see if it's *the* Patrick Amaranth and not just someone impersonating him. But when I go to his profile, it looks like the real deal. He's big in the tech world, with almost five hundred thousand followers. How did someone like him even find my page?

Holy crap! This is amazing, and it only proves that my strategy is working. If I can get someone like him to shout out my page, then I'll pass Tanner in no time. I look through his photos, and while most of them are of different computers and new phone models, there are some of Patrick himself, too. He's probably in his early thirties and is slim with a shaved head. What he's lacking in hair, however, he more than makes up for with his massive beard.

I've never been into bearded guys, but it kind of suits him. He's smiling in all his pictures, giving him a warm and friendly look. Surely, someone like him would want to help out a smaller creator. I have to strike while the iron is hot, but I'm not sure how to go about this. Do I just slide into his DMs and ask for a shout-out? That seems kind of crappy, like I'm just using him. I mean, I *am*, but I don't want *him* to think that. I need to establish some sort of a connection first.

I follow him back and like his most recent post. Best to start out slow. I decide to post something, too, just to see if he interacts with my post at all. If he does, then I'll message him.

It's just a selfie; I need to get something up quick. I'm winking at the camera, smiling, and as it gets uploaded onto my feed, I watch my notifications closely. A couple of likes trickle in, but nothing from Patrick so far. I need to give it some time, I tell myself. He's probably busy. It's not like he's just sitting there watching my feed for updates.

I make myself put the phone down and do some cleaning around my apartment. Every time I pass my phone, I pick it up, just to check. Then after an hour, it happens. Patrick Amaranth has liked my post! I squeal, jumping around. Here we go; the ball is rolling.

I consider messaging him, but I feel like I need to build up to that.

So, over the next few days, I keep uploading as I usually would. I like and comment on Patrick's posts as well, and he likes my photos. When he uploads a review for the latest phone from a new brand, I comment on it.

This looks great. I really enjoy reading your reviews. It's a jungle out there with all the different models coming out. Mind if I ask you some questions about this one?

I don't know if this is the right approach, but I need to move things along. If he thinks I actually care about tech stuff, then he might be more open to telling his followers about me. I get a thumbs up in response, so I take that as a *yes*. I'm just about to type out a message for him when I get a notification that Patrick Amaranth has messaged me first. I smile.

Heard you were interested in the DX-1 model, he writes. *What do you want to know?*

I think for a second, then I start typing. *What's the camera like?*

Patrick gets back to me right away. *It's really impressive, actually. You take a lot of pictures, don't you?*

All the time, I write. *Would you say the quality is better than the camera I'm using for my photos now?* I want him to look at my pictures; they seem to appeal to other guys, at least. Hopefully, they appeal to Patrick, too. Why else would he follow me?

Your pictures look pretty great, to be honest.

A wide grin draws across my face. Hook, line, and sinker. *Yeah? Which one is your favorite?*

It takes him a moment to answer, but then three

little dots appear. *I like the Christmas-themed ones. Really puts me in the holiday spirit.*

I frown. I have a few pictures of me around town, posing in front of Santa statues and reindeers. There are some images of me in a skimpy outfit with a Santa hat, too. Maybe he means those.

Are you into Christmas? I could probably do some shots around town for you, if that's something you think your followers would like.

I bite my lip, waiting. I really hope he takes me up on my offer.

I don't know; it doesn't really fit my brand. Feels kind of random to have you just pop up on my feed.

We could do some sort of collaboration then, I write. *I could pose with whatever thing you're reviewing next. We could even meet up if you want. You'd be Santa, and I'd be your helper.* I add in a winky face for good measure.

I don't think so, but thanks. Our stuff are just too different. Don't get me wrong, I really like your pictures. It's just not what I do on my page.

Crap. I take a deep breath. I can't get mad. I need to keep him on my side for this to work. *Got it,* I write. *No problem at all. So, got anything fun going on for the holiday?*

We message back and forth for a bit, then Patrick tells me that he has a meeting. I toss my phone onto my couch, groaning loudly. I really thought that would work. But I can't give up now, not when I finally opened up a line of communication with someone as big as Patrick Amaranth.

I guess I'll have to play it slow.

$\mathcal{I}$ have a post that pops off a few days later. I get more likes on it than I've gotten on any other picture, and as I walk into work, I have four new DMs from guys I don't think are bots. My posts are actually reaching people! I don't have time to check what they've written though, because Eric is waiting for me right by the doors of the store.

"Good morning," I say, not liking the expression on his pudgy face. His glasses are sitting low on his nose, making him look like an angry little school librarian.

"Well, that's debatable, isn't it?" Eric remarks and glares at me. I frown, wondering what his problem is.

"Is everything okay?" I ask, my heart starting to pick up speed.

"Let's go into my office," he responds and gestures for me to follow him. He doesn't wait for me to answer; he just starts walking off. I hurry after him; he's pretty fast for someone so short.

Eric tells me to close the door behind me when we walk into the tiny room he calls an office, and I sit down on a wooden stool in front of his desk.

"So," I say and clasp my hands together, "what do you want to talk to me about?"

"Sophie," he starts solemnly, "how long have you been working here?"

I think back, and I'm horrified at the answer. "Almost seven years." God, this was just supposed to be a temporary thing after high school. Something to do while I figured out what I want to do with my life. I can't believe it's been seven years already.

"Seven years," Eric repeats, "and do you think it's been a good seven years?"

Where is he going with this? "Sure, I mean… yes. It's been fine."

"Yes, I think *fine* is a good way to describe your time here," Eric speaks with a nod. "You are a perfectly fine employee. No more, no less. But over the past few months, I've really noticed a decline in your performance."

"Look, if this is about me being late a few times, then—"

"It's not just that," he interrupts. "You shelf things in the wrong place, you take too long completing simple tasks, and you can sometimes be quite snippy with the customers."

Only when they're being idiots, I almost say, but I hold my tongue. "Okay, I'm sorry. I'll do better."

"That's just the thing," Eric replies. "This isn't the first time we've had this talk, is it? You haven't improved despite being written up several times. I think I've given you a fair amount of leeway, Sophie. I've given you plenty of chances to improve. But I'm afraid that comes to an end today.

Shit. This can't be happening! Not now. "Are you firing me, Eric?" I hear a slight tremor in my voice, but I don't care. He can't fire me! I just bought a really nice tripod for my camera. I can't afford to lose my income!

But my boss slowly nods his head. "I'm afraid I am, yes. This just isn't working out anymore. You can collect your final paycheck at the end of the week, and I expect you to turn in your keys then as well. You can go home now, Sophie."

"But who will cover my shift?" I ask.

"I've hired a new girl," Eric says. "I think she'll fit in great here."

Oh my god. I just got fired! I've never worked

anywhere else in my life, and I never went to college! There's no way I'll be able to get a job somewhere else. Who the hell would hire someone like me? I don't even know where to begin looking for another job. There aren't very many options in town. Am I going to have to do some crazy commute? Or worse, move altogether? I've always lived here, and even though I give the town a lot of crap, it's my home. I don't want to leave.

I run into Lacey on my way out. She winces when she sees my face.

"So, it's true?" she asks. "He fired you?"

"You knew about this?" I ask, sounding a bit harsher than I had intended.

"I didn't know, honest! I'm sorry, Sophie."

"Yeah, well, sorry doesn't pay the bills," I mutter. "Damn it! I don't know what to do."

"You could go back to school," Lacey suggests. "This could be a blessing in disguise."

School? With what money? "Yeah, maybe," I respond quietly, "or I'll have to start selling feet pics online."

"See!" She laughs and smiles. "You've got a plan."

"Ha-ha." I glare at her. "Seriously, I don't know what to do."

"I can ask my mom if she needs extra help at the souvenir shop over the holiday season," she suggests. "What do you say?"

I hate the thought of working in Lacey's mom's

little store, but it's better than nothing. "Okay." I finally give in. "Thanks."

This is the worst day ever! I'm not even upset about losing the job; it's the money I'm worried about. I head back outside and get into my car. I just sit there for a moment, taking everything in. Seven years. I worked at this shitty grocery store for seven fucking years. I might not be the model employee, but Eric has some gall just firing me like that. Like my long and dutiful service at his crappy store doesn't mean anything at all.

Well, maybe not so dutiful. But I always show up for my shifts; that has to count for something.

What am I supposed to do for money now? Even if I do get a job at Lacey's mom's dumb shop, I can't imagine the pay being as good as my old job. *Damn it.*

I drive back home, barely noticing where I'm going. Then I pace around my living room for almost an hour, trying to think things through. I grab my laptop and search for any job listing I can find in the area.

There are only three jobs available in town. One is for a teaching position at the local high school; I'm way underqualified for that. The second is a plumbing job, so that's not happening, either. The third and last job listing is for a caretaker position at the local old folks' home. I really, really don't want to do that, but it seems like it's my only option, unless I want to look for a job outside of town.

Next, I need a resume. I've never written a resume

in my life. I just asked for the job at the grocery store when I was the young age of nineteen and was hired on the spot. I've never had to actually *apply* for a job before. I look up templates for resumes online and start filling in my information.

The page is pathetically empty. A high school degree and seven years at the local grocery store. Not exactly impressive. Still, I send in my application. No harm in trying.

But I need another plan, just in case this job falls through. I look at my phone. Tanner is making money through his social media. Why can't I? He regularly has sponsors; I can get myself some of those. I look through some of his collaborations, and I choose a company that sells jewelry. I find a contact form on their website and start writing my pitch, and telling them how I have thousands of followers with great engagement.

That part isn't necessarily true, I guess. I mostly get engagement from the different guys who seem to enjoy my pictures. Desperate times call for desperate measures, and I need to do what I can to bring some money in. After I send in my pitch, I feel quite accomplished. I didn't just let myself wallow in my anxiety about losing my job; that's good. Now I just have to wait for the company to get back to me.

To distract myself, I put on a cute outfit and do my hair and makeup. I take some selfies as I'm lounging on my couch, showing off my legs in my short skirt. The pictures turn out really cute, and I pick one of them to post. I get a message from DonnieWylde93 right away. Seriously, does he not do anything else other than check his social media?

I keep thinking about the other day, he writes to me. I know he wants a repeat performance. I also know he wants pictures. It *was* kind of fun; I liked being desired like that. I type out a reply.

Yeah? What are you thinking about?

You know what I'm thinking about, sweetheart. I wouldn't mind doing that again.

I hesitate. I'm not exactly in the mood for that sort of thing. *Yeah, sorry. I think that was just a one-time thing for me.*

Are you sure? Maybe I should just come over to your place. Show you a good time in person. He sends a winky face.

For a moment, I imagine what it would be like having him here. Seeing if he would live up to his big words in his messages. I haven't been with anyone in a while. Donnie keeps sending messages about coming over, how good we'd be together. Would it be stupid to invite him over? Probably, but I'm not feeling particularly smart today. I just want to be distracted from everything that's happened. My fingers hover over the screen, then I write the words.

Alright. Come over.

CHAPTER 9

It takes exactly an hour before there's a knock on my door. Donnie must have gotten in his car right away after I sent the message. Weirdly enough, I'm not nervous. There's this strange sense of anticipation inside me, though.

When I open the door, we're almost at eye level. Donnie is just slightly taller than me, but his shoulders are broad, and I can clearly see the muscle definition under his tight shirt. Okay, I can work with this.

"Hey, sweetheart," he says and grins at me. "About time we did this."

"Yeah, I guess," I say back to him and step to the side. "Come in."

Donnie waltzes through my doorway and looks around the apartment. "You've got a pretty nice place here."

"Thanks, I moved in last year. Do you want something to drink?"

Donnie shakes his head. "I'm not here for drinks." He looks me up and down, and I can see him breathing heavily as he does so. He's getting excited already.

Okay, this is it. I'm actually going to sleep with him, with some stranger I met online not that long ago. This is probably stupid, but he's already here, and I really want to do it. That's what it all boils down to in the end.

"You're wearing the same skirt as in your picture," he remarks when he notices my outfit, coming closer to me. He's standing right in front of me, his fingers stroking up and down the side of my right leg until it reaches the hem of my skirt. I shiver as he's touching my bare leg. "Did you wear this just for me?"

"Yeah, I did," I flirt back, even though that's not even close to being true. "Do you like it?"

Donnie snickers. "I love it. We should take some more pics of you in it. I can promote you on my feed again if you want."

"Yeah?" I ask. "You'd do that?"

The look he gives me is heated, and the grip on my legs tightens. He slides his hands up to my waist, and then he cups my breasts through my shirt. Donnie drags a thumb over one hardening nipple, and I gasp.

"Of course, I would," he mutters with a heavy breath, his voice practically a growl by this point. "We'll set it up later. I want you first, sweetheart. Is that alright?"

I nod, then I lead him into my bedroom and lie down on top of the covers. He's just standing there for a moment looking at me, absentmindedly rubbing his bulge through his jeans.

"Well?" I ask. "Are you going to come over to me, or just stand there?"

"In a minute. Take off your clothes first," he says, his voice low.

I do. First my top, then I shimmy out of my skirt. Donnie unbuttons his jeans, and I see all of him. He's not even wearing any boxers! I get out of my panties, lying there naked before him. Donnie moans deep in his throat as he's looking at me, stroking himself.

In a second, he strips, getting out of the rest of his clothes in record speed. He *does* look pretty good naked. If it weren't for the smug look on his face, telling me that he's well aware of the fact that he looks good naked, then he might even be hot.

Donnie crawls on top of me, takes one nipple into his mouth, and sucks on it hard. I hiss; it's a weird mix of pleasure and pain, and I'm not sure if I like that.

He moves on and kisses his way down my stomach, and then he licks and bites on my inner thighs. My breathing picks up as he starts touching me, teasing my most sensitive spot with slow strokes of his fingers.

"You ready, sweetheart?"

I nod, not quite finding my voice in the moment. Donnie leans in, and I moan as he puts his mouth on me. He pushes a finger inside as he licks and sucks, and I raise my hips to meet his touch. Donnie adds another finger and picks up his pace. Within the next minute, he's pretty much jackhammering me down there. I place a hand in his hair, and his eyes meet mine.

"Slow down," I tell him, my voice coming out husky and hoarse.

"Women always love it when I go fast," he whispers, then returns to licking me the same as before. I frown.

"Donnie, slow down."

He sighs. "Fine." Then he winks at me. "Someone's bossy. I like it."

Bossy? For telling him to go slow? He really is an ass. But at least he's returned to a pace that actually feels good, so I lie back down and close my eyes. Might as well get an orgasm out of this.

He picks up the pace again, and after a few more licks, he stops altogether. "Did you cum?"

Did he just ask me if I came? "I think you'd notice if I did," I respond sarcastically.

"My jaw is getting tired," he whines. "I'll make

you cum later though, promise. I just really need to be inside you. I'm going crazy over here."

Might as well just get to it. I wanted to have sex, so I'm going to have sex. I can get myself off later if I have to. "There are condoms in the nightstand drawer."

He reaches over and opens the small drawer. He rips open a packet and rolls the condom over his hard length, hissing as he drags a hand up and down his erection a few times. Why do I get the feeling that this is going to be over quickly?

Donnie settles between my legs, and I feel him at my entrance. I relax as he pushes inside, and it takes a moment for me to adjust to his size. Donnie groans, his whole body tensing up as he's buried inside of me. For a moment, I'm afraid he's cum already, disappointment rushing through my body. But then he starts to move, hips rolling, hitting my most sensitive spot as he thrusts in and out.

"Yeah, that's it," he pants. "So ready for me. So tight."

His eyes are clamped shut, and it's almost like he's talking to himself rather than talking to me. I don't care. I arch up to meet his thrusts, and that seems to set him off. Donnie moves faster, groaning loudly every time he pushes into me. His face is all red, and there's a vein popping out on the side of his neck.

I reach between us and touch myself. If I want to find release, I'm going to have to do it myself. He does feel good inside me, but it's not enough. He goes even faster, and I gasp as I get into the perfect rhythm with my fingers. I fall over the edge soon enough, crying out and bucking up as my orgasm explodes in my body.

Donnie curses loudly and hammers into me, and then his whole body stiffens. His jaw is slack as he ejaculates, a desperate sound escaping his lips before he collapses on top of me. He's heavy, but I wrap my legs around him anyway, needing the closeness as I come down from my orgasm.

"That was so good," he mutters, voice low. "You felt so good, sweetheart."

I don't say anything. It was alright, nothing to write home about. Donnie props himself up and looks at me, looking far too pleased with himself. I raise an eyebrow.

"What?"

"Told you I'd take you there."

I almost laugh. *I* got myself over the edge; he had very little to do with it. Now that I think about it, I could have achieved the same thing on my own. Why did I invite him over again? A moment of weakness. Maybe it won't be a total waste, though. Not if he's going to post one of my pictures again.

Donnie is circling one of my nipples with a feathery light touch, making my skin break out into goosebumps. I can feel him getting excited again. Damn, that's a quick recovery. I'll give him that.

Without a word, Donnie pushes inside me again. This time, he goes slow, kissing my neck and breathing heavily into my ear. This is better; this is actually pretty nice. He keeps talking, keeps telling me how good it feels. I rake my fingers over his back, and he bites down on my neck, sucking hard as his movements become more erratic. His whole body jerks, and then he ejaculates again.

A low sound fills the room, a deep groan that seems to be coming from his very core. He rolls off of me in the next second, eyes closed and chest heaving. I'm left very much unsatisfied, and I almost expect him to get back to me once he comes down from his high. That's hoping for too much, though. Donnie props himself up onto his elbow and looks me over.

"You know, I have a bit of an audience on different platforms. I could get your pics out there too if you want."

"What kind of platforms?" I ask, not sure I'll like his answer.

"You know," he says and wiggles his eyebrow. "It's very classy. I don't want you to think it's something dirty. Mostly just lingerie; maybe some topless action. Are you interested?"

I gape at him. "You're asking me to do porn? Are you serious?"

"It's not *porn*," he corrects me, sounding a bit annoyed all of a sudden. "It's just nudes. You'd be great at it; it's not that different from what you're already posting. It would really rack up your following."

I can practically hear my heart beating faster and

faster as my pulse rushes through me. "No way!" I almost yell. "Forget it."

This isn't fun anymore. Donnie definitely isn't worth the boost in followers. I just want him to leave. I sit up and wrap my blanket around me. "I think you should leave.

Donnie sits up now, too. "Why are you being a bitch? I thought we were having a good time."

"Get. Out."

Without another word, Donnie gets out of bed, grabbing his clothes. He gives me one last look, and then he leaves the bedroom. I hear the front door slam shut a few seconds later. This was a mistake. I lie back down, closing my eyes. Tanner's face flashes in my mind. I don't want to think about him, but I can't help but think that this would have been so much better if it had been him here and not Donnie.

Stop thinking about him! I mentally scold myself. I decide I'm going to block Donnie. I don't want to interact with him anymore. I'll keep to actual decent people, like Patrick Amaranth. I can still get him to promote my page. I'm sure of it.

When I grab my phone to block Donnie, I see that he has already unfollowed me. I can't help but laugh.

Good riddance.

few days later, I wake up to an email from the jewelry company I contacted a while back. They want to send me a few things. I squeal, reading that part again. I have a sponsor! Then I get to the part about compensation. They write that there is no budget for monetary compensation, but I will get a ten percent discount code to share with my follow-ers. My excitement dies down. No money. I decide to accept anyway. We all have to start somewhere, right? And I do get some jewelry out of this.

I guess my following is still too small for any deals that actually pay. I've been tempted to buy more followers, but my bank account is looking quite pathetic at the moment, so I hold off. Maybe after I've paid this month's rent, I can get some more. In the meantime, I continue to talk to Patrick, just keeping the conversation light and friendly. But I do need to give another shot with him, and figure out a way to get him to mention me to his followers.

I send the jewelry company my address and go to my closet to find something to wear for the day. I want to shoot some pictures outside today, change things up from the images I take inside my apartment. I choose a beige dress that hits me about mid-thigh, and I pair it with some boots that hit me just below the hem of the dress. It's cute and sexy, all at once.

It's snowing again when I go outside, and my mood goes sour. Damn it, it's going to get my hair all wet. I didn't even put on a hat! I'll have to work quickly then.

There's a massive reindeer in the middle of downtown, and I set up my camera in front of it. Patrick is going to like this, I'm sure of it. Maybe I'll send him the picture before I upload it, just to get his opinion.

People are giving me weird looks as I pose and snap my pictures, but I don't care. I see some teenagers snicker as they walk past me, but I just keep going. An old man stops and glances at me, and then at my camera.

"I can take some pictures for you, dear," he says, reaching for my camera. I don't even have time to tell him no before he bumps it, and it falls to the ground. I think the snow softened the fall a little, but there's still a horrible crashing sound as it lands. He looks horrified, trying to bend down to pick it up.

"I've got it!" I practically scream at him, trying not to sound angry, even though I'm seething inside. Who just grabs another person's property like that?

"I didn't mean to...," he mumbles, his voice weak and shaking.

I smile at him. I don't need a crying man to take care of when my brand-new camera is all wet from the snow. "It's okay; it was an accident. I should probably get this inside, though."

I don't wait for him to say anything else. I just grab my things and go. *Crap, crap, crap!* I try to get the camera to turn back on, but it's not working. The lens is a little dented, and there's a small crack running across the display. Why did he have to touch it? Now I have to get it fixed, and God knows I don't have the money for that! I haven't even had it for very long, and it's already broken! Just great!

The closest place to me is the coffee shop, so I rush in there and head for their restroom. I do my best to dry the camera off, but the damage is already done. *Damn it.* I go back outside, and as I walk by the cash register, the girl working there calls out to me, a sour look on her face.

"Hey, are you going to buy anything? The restroom is for customers only."

I'm tempted to tell her to get lost, but then there's a man's voice behind me.

"Aren't you that girl?"

I turn around, and a young man is standing right behind me. He's probably a few years younger than me, about twenty-two or twenty-three. Kind of cute. Tall as hell.

"That girl?" I ask.

"Yeah, I think I follow you." He picks up his phone, and after some scrolling, he shows me one of my pictures. "It is you, isn't it?"

I nod and smile at him. "Yeah, that's me."

"That's so cool. I really like your content." His dark eyes settle on my chest for a moment, so I know exactly what he likes about my content. Honestly, I don't mind.

"Well, thanks," I tell him. "I should probably—"

"Can I buy you a coffee?" he interrupts. "Unless you already have plans."

I hesitate. A cute guy wants to buy me coffee. Might be just what I need after what happened outside. "Okay," I give in. "Let's grab a coffee."

A blush spreads across his cheeks, and he scrambles for his wallet. It's kind of cute how flustered he's getting, just because he recognized me from my profile. "What do you want?"

"Latte," I say. "Extra foam."

He puts in our order while I go find us a table. Quickly, I search through my followers, hoping to see a profile picture that looks like him. I find him after just a minute, and I see that he's a gamer. Not a massive following, but there are a few hundred people there, at least.

I stash my phone away when he joins me at the table and hands me my latte. I smile at him, and he's blushing again. He keeps looking between my face and my chest, and I sit up straighter to give him a better view. The blush never leaves his face, and he just keeps saying how much he likes my pictures.

"What's your name?" I ask.

"Sam," he says, his blush deepening. Damn, he's really nervous! It probably makes me a jerk, but I love watching him squirm like that.

"It's nice to meet you, Sam," I greet him, keeping my tone light. I lean forward, and his eyes instantly fall to my cleavage. I see him swallow hard, and then he takes a big sip from his mug. This is kind of fun.

"Um…" He clears his throat. "Yeah, it's really cool to meet you, too. I only found your profile last week. You're really pretty."

"Thank you," I say, smiling wide. "So, what do you do?"

"Me?" He looks even more flustered. "Um, I work just outside of town. I'm an IT consultant."

I raise an eyebrow. "That's pretty cool. How old are you? You must have just finished school."

"I graduated in the summer," he tells me. "I'm twenty-two."

So, I was right about his age. I can see him working in IT; he looks kind of nerdy. Checks out with his gaming content, too. Maybe that's a stereotype, but he fits the bill. "Do you like it?"

He shrugs. "It's a pretty good job. I'm saving up to get my own place, but it's so expensive. Here in town as well; even the apartments are overpriced."

Does he still live with his parents? That must suck. "Yeah, I was pretty lucky when I found my place," I say. "It's not too bad."

"How long have you lived there?"

"Only about a year. I shared a place with a friend before that."

"Must be nice," Sam smiles, "to have a place of your own."

"It is," I respond with a smile back. "Can't be easy to still be living with your parents, though. You can't exactly bring home any girls."

His eyes widen slightly. "No, I can't."

I lean over the table even more. His eyes are bulging. It's like he's never seen a pair of breasts before. "Must be frustrating. I would go crazy."

"Yeah, it's…" He swallows hard. "It can be sometimes."

I tilt my head, feeling bold under his gaze. I don't know what it is, but Sam's obvious appreciation for me is intoxicating. I still can't believe he recognized me from my profile! With all the bots, it's sometimes hard to remember that there are actual people among my followers, too. "What is it you like about my pictures, Sam?"

He's squirming in his seat. "I just think they're… nice."

"In what way?"

"The way you look in them," he says, the words barely more than a whisper.

I glance down at my dress. "Do you like my clothes?"

"Yeah."

"I have a bunch more back home," I whisper to him, smiling at the way his entire body tenses. "You want to help me pick out what to wear in my next picture? We could take some pictures together, too. I'm sure I can bring some people over to your profile."

"Really?" he asks, stunned. "You'd do that?"

And maybe you can bring over some people to mine, I think, but I keep my mouth shut. One step at a time. I nod. "Sure. What do you say?"

I love the eagerness in his eyes as he nods. Sam's so different from Donnie's cocky way of being around me. I think I like this better. I eat up the way he's admiring me when I stand up.

"Let's go."

CHAPTER 11

Sam is quiet when I let us into my apartment. He looks a bit unsure of what to do, just standing there in the hallway in his coat and boots. I shrug out of my jacket and smile at him.

"Make yourself at home."

"Okay." He takes off his coat and hangs it next to mine. Damn, he really *is* tall.

"Do you want something to drink?" I ask and make my way into the kitchen.

"Maybe some water," Sam says and follows me inside. I hand him a glass, and he gulps down the cold water.

"You don't have to be nervous, Sam," I tell him. "I'm just a regular person."

He smiles a bashful smile, then his dark eyes meet mine. "Okay, sorry. It's just weird seeing you in real life."

It's surreal to have someone recognize me like this. To have someone know things about me without having met me before. But at the same time, it's really cool. If I can get in contact with more people like Sam, then I won't need to buy any more bots. Hopefully, I can get to the bigger fish eventually, but I'll take what I can get. Sam's small following is nothing to sneeze at, either.

"So," I begin, "I need an outfit for my next picture. Let's go pick it out."

Sam is right on my heel as I make my way to my closet. He's standing so close that our arms are brushing against each other. "You have a lot of clothes," he comments, carefully touching one of my dresses. "Hey, I recognize this one!" he exclaims and pulls out the red dress I wore a while back.

"Yeah? You like that one?"

He nods. "It looked nice on you."

"Well, let me try it on for you."

Sam's mouth hangs open as I unzip my dress and let it fall to the floor. I pretend I don't see the way his eyes roam over my body, that I don't notice the way he's covering up his crotch with his hands. I put on the dress and turn my back to him.

"Would you mind zipping me up?"

His hands are cold as they graze against my skin. He pulls the zipper up slowly, and I can feel his breath on the back of my neck. He's practically panting. I whirl around, showing off the dress for him.

"What do you think?"

He nods. "Yeah. It's very nice."

I pout, looking like I'm thinking really hard. "But I've already worn it in a picture. I think we need something else. See what else you can find in there."

He turns back to my closet and picks out a top that still has the tag on. It's cropped, and only has thin spaghetti straps to keep it in place. "How about this one?"

I take it from him, holding it up against my body. "Yeah, this one is nice. I could wear this in our picture; it kind of matches your shirt. It'll look good." I grab a pair of jeans and shimmy into them. Then I have Sam unzip my dress again, and I slip on the sheer top.

A low moan escapes his lips, and he reaches new shades of red as I show him the outfit. "You look really nice," he compliments me.

"Thanks, you're sweet. Should we take that picture?"

He nods slowly. "Okay. Um… I'm not usually in the pictures on my page. You might have to guide me a little."

"Sure," I mouth and smile. I grab my phone and tell him to follow me into the living room. I wish I had my camera instead, but it's still broken.

I try to think about how to do this. Whenever I talk to Patrick Amaranth, he's always yammering on about his brand. I don't think Sam cares much about that though, but I guess it can't hurt to play into the gamer content he's got going on. I'm not supposed to know about that though, so I tilt my head and ask him, "Can you show me your profile? I just want to see what type of picture would go with your feed."

"That doesn't matter," he says. "It's enough to have you in the picture."

"Okay, if you're sure." I sit down on the couch. "Let's keep it simple then. How about a selfie?"

"Sure, we can do a selfie," he replies and sits down next to me. Our legs are touching, and it's pretty obvious that he's nervous. If I'd known my page was going to have *this* type of impression on people, I would have started sooner.

"You okay?" I ask coyly. "You look a little flustered, Sam."

"I'm okay. How should we do this?"

I hold up my phone at a slight angle and tell him to smile. I deliberately get closer, so that I'm pressed to his side. I feel him put his arm around my back, and I snap the picture.

"Let's do one more, just in case," I tell him and take a couple more. I then pull the photos up on the screen and flip through them. "This one's pretty good," I say and hand him my phone. "What do you think?"

We're both smiling, although Sam is looking a little shaken. He nods and gives me the phone back.

"You're so beautiful," he says, the words barely even audible. I smile sweetly.

"Oh, please. You're just saying that."

"No," he says again, his voice firm. "I mean it; you're amazing."

This guy is like a puppy! I could probably tell him the sky is pink, and he'd believe me. "Thank you. You're a really nice guy, Sam."

His gaze flicks between my eyes and my lips, and I feel a flutter in the pit of my stomach. Sam leans in closer, his eyes hooded and his breathing labored.

"Can I kiss you?"

"Alright," I whisper, and not even a second later, his lips are on mine. It's a hard and eager sort of kiss, and I have to push on his chest a little to stop him from crushing me entirely. His tongue is fighting with mine, swirling around like a tumble dryer. I don't think Sam has a lot of experience kissing women with the way he's going at my mouth. I push at his chest again, and he pulls away.

"Did I do something wrong?" he asks.

I shake my head with a smile. "No, you're fine. Just slow down a little, and let me enjoy you."

He groans and captures my lips again. This time, he's gentler, exploring me with soft, languid kisses. I wrap my arms around his neck and press closer.

That's more like it. His hold on me is gentle, like he's afraid he's going to break me. I pull him down over me as I lie back onto the couch, and that seems to make Sam bolder.

One hand is caressing my breast through the sheer fabric of the top, and he's pressing himself against me, his excitement clear as day. It's nice, but it doesn't take long before I get kind of bored. This is how I used to feel about kissing until Tanner showed me how great it can be.

As soon as Tanner comes to my mind, I'm over it all. Sam's hand is gracing the edge of my jeans, but I don't want to sleep with him. Not anymore. Images of Tanner and Donnie and Sam whirl together in my head, and I push at him slightly. Sam is looking dazed as he blinks down at me, his cheeks flushed.

"Is something wrong?" he asks. I shake my head.

"No, I'm okay. I just think we need to put on the brakes. I… I just remembered that I have plans to go see my mom."

It's the first thing that pops into my head, but Sam seems to be buying it. He sits up, helping me get up as well. "Oh, okay. No problem. Maybe we can see each other some other time then?"

I hesitate. Sam is a sweet guy, but I have absolutely no interest in seeing him again. I still want him to post the picture, though. "Sure, we'll see."

His face brightens. "Great!"

"You okay?" I ask, feeling kind of bad to have just cut things short like this.

"More than okay," he says with a smile. "That was amazing. I can't believe I got to kiss you. I've been fantasizing about what it would be like ever since I found your profile."

"You have?"

He nods. "I love your pictures, but they're nothing compared to the real thing." He turns to me, kissing me gently, holding my face like I'm something precious. "Send me that photo, and I'll upload it when I get back home."

I find his profile and send him a DM with the photo of us. He stares down at it with a fond expression on his face.

I smile. I mean, it's a bit weird that he seems so attached to me just because he follows my page, and we only just met today! But at the same time, I can see myself getting used to something like this. Having people view me in the same light as Sam does can be kind of cool.

Sam's still sitting next to me, smiling as if I've just given him an early Christmas present or something. I smile back, raising my eyebrows.

"Right, so… gotta get to my mom's place soon."

"Are you going to do something fun?" he asks.

Is he for real? "Not really," I just say. "Just… visiting."

It takes him forever to finally take the hint and leave. I keep an eye on my notifications to see if he has tagged me in the picture of the two of us, and when it finally happens, I instantly go over to his page to check the likes and comments. There's not a lot there yet, but just thirty minutes later, I have three new followers that came from Sam's page. Better than nothing, but I kind of regret inviting him over.

I should probably stop doing that. Donnie was a monumental mistake, and Sam is probably going to get hurt when he finds out that I don't want to see him again. I should focus on what's important instead of screwing around with random guys.

I'm making great strides toward my goal, and I'm getting a bit closer to Tanner's numbers day by day. I might need another boost of followers soon, but I'm going to really hunker down and try to get that shout-out from Patrick Amaranth. I know I can do it! I just need to frame it in a way that makes it seem like it's beneficial for him, too.

I pace around the room, trying to think. I should contact some tech company, see if I can get some products sent my way. Then I would definitely fit in with Patrick's brand, and he'd *have* to agree to some sort of collaboration… if I can manage something like that.

CHAPTER 12

It costs almost as much to fix my camera as it did to buy it in the first place, but at least it's working again. I'm burning through my bank account, however, and I start looking for jobs outside of town. I send a pitch to some tech companies for sponsorships, too, determined to snag one that will catch Patrick's eye. So far, I've got nothing, but I refuse to give up.

I constantly check my email to see if the old folks'

home has gotten back to me, but there's never anything there. Not surprised, though; I don't have any relevant experience. It *did* say in the ad that whoever got hired would receive training on the job, so it probably wasn't anything too complicated.

WHEN ANOTHER TWO days have passed, I decide to give them a call. I'm starting to get desperate, and in a moment of weakness last night, I bought some more followers. I just needed to cheer myself up, but I definitely regret it today.

A cheerful voice picks up on the other end. "Welcome to the North Pole Home for Seniors! How can I help you?"

I take a deep breath, suddenly nervous. "Hi, my name is Sophie Leigh. I applied for a position with you a little while back, and I just wanted to know if the role has been filled."

"Oh, hello!" the woman says as if I've just given her the most wonderful news. "It hasn't been filled yet, no. I think my boss was actually about to contact you for an interview, Sophie. Isn't that fun?"

"Really?" I ask eagerly, bouncing on the edge of my seat. "That's great!"

"I'll have her call you as soon as possible, and the two of you can set something up. How does that sound?"

"That would be great," I respond. "Thank you! Thank you so much!"

"No problem at all, darling. You have a nice day, alright?"

"You, too."

A warm, fuzzy feeling settles in my stomach. What a nice woman! For the first time in a while, my money situation doesn't feel so bad. Maybe things will work out after all. I just have to get this job, and then I'll be able to get more things to help my social media along.

I GET the call that same afternoon. A woman with a no-nonsense sort of voice greets me on the other end.

"So, I've been looking over your application, Sophie—" she says, and I immediately cut in.

"I know there's not a lot on there, but—"

"No, don't you worry about that. I actually really liked that you'd been working at the same company for so long. That kind of loyalty is hard to come by these days."

Yeah, *that's* why I stayed at the grocery store for so long. Loyalty. "I'm glad to hear that."

"You would obviously need some training, but that's no problem. You wouldn't actually do anything that has to do with our clients' medical care, except for some basic things. Distributing medicine and things like that. This role is mostly a caretaking one. You would keep them company. Help them get dressed and feel put together. Our clients really value that sort of thing; it makes them feel like themselves."

"That sounds wonderful!"

"I'd like to meet you, of course," she continues, "see if we're a good fit together. But if we are, then I think you'd be a great addition to our little team."

My stomach flutters at her words. "Great! Looking forward to it."

"Is tomorrow good? I have some time before lunch if you're available."

"Tomorrow is perfect," I say, grinning wide. I have an interview. I have a freaking interview!

"Lovely," she says. "I'll see you then."

I can't believe it! I might actually get a job; I won't have to sell all my valuables. I dance toward my closet and try to pick out what to wear for my interview. None of my new clothes are really appropriate, so I look through my old ones. I've barely touched them since I started posting pictures online, and it feels a little weird when I try on a dark pair of pants with a button-down shirt. I throw a navy knitted sweater on top, giving me a put-together, preppy sort of look. If I pull my hair up into a ponytail and just do a light sweeping of makeup, I think that makes me look fairly professional.

Pleased with my choice, I put the clothes back in the closet for tomorrow and go sit down on my couch. My pomeranian jumps up on my lap and begins to lick my hands as I pull out my phone. I have a new DM from Sam. He's been messaging me nonstop ever since I invited him over. I keep my answers short, hoping he'll take the hint.

For a moment, I wonder if this is what Tanner felt with me before he broke things off. But that was different; we were *actually* dating. Sam's just a random guy I made out with a little. There's no need for him to constantly message me like this.

Can I see you again?

It's not the first time he has asked that question. I keep deflecting, telling him I'm busy. But maybe it's time to just nip this in the butt. I start to write out a message, only to delete it all again. I don't know how to do this without being mean. Best to just rip off the bandage. He's a grown man; he can take it.

Sam, I really enjoyed meeting you, but I'm just not looking for anything right now. I think it's best if we don't see each other again, and just let that day be a fond memory for us both. I hope you understand.

Does that sound weird? Maybe that part about it being a fond memory is a bit much. Whatever, at least I've made myself clear. A new message appears.

But I think I've fallen for you, Sophie.

Oookay. I stare at his message, eyes wide. What the hell? Is he being serious? I don't even know what to say. Do I even answer him?

You're not falling for me, Sam. You don't even know me.

Three little dots show up at once. *I've never felt so close to another person before. You can't just throw this away.*

That's a little intense. We spent two, maybe three, hours together. Surely, he's just exaggerating. But then again, he did seem quite inexperienced. Maybe I'm the first woman to have ever shown him any type of attention. And now he's imprinted on me or something, like a baby duck. I should let him down easy, but I also don't want to drag it out. It's better that he lets go of his little fantasy of me and move on. He's so sweet, and he good-looking, too. Someone like him shouldn't have a problem finding a girlfriend.

I'm sorry, Sam. I don't feel the same. You're a great guy. I'm sure you'll find someone else before you know it. I promise.

I stare at the screen for almost ten minutes, waiting for a reply. I don't get one. Maybe that's for the best. What a fucking mess.

I STILL FEEL bad when I get ready for my interview the next day, but I force myself to focus on something other than Sam. He'll get over it. Right now, I need to ace this interview. I can't be distracted like this.

The drive over to the North Pole Home for Seniors only takes a few minutes, and I park right outside the big building. I've never really noticed it before, even though I know I've gone past it many times. It's kind of grand, actually. Old, but carefully looked after. I get out of my car and take a deep breath. Okay, showtime.

A smiling woman around my mom's age greets me behind the front desk down in the lobby. She's round and plump with kind eyes, and I realize that this is the person I had spoken to on the phone.

"You must be Sophie," she says before I get a chance to introduce myself. "It's so nice to meet you. My name is Rachel, and if you need anything at all, just let me know."

"It's nice to meet you, Rachel," I greet her and smile.

The corners of my mouth are shaking a little. Now that I'm here, I find myself more nervous than I thought I would be.

"Pauline will be with you in just a moment. You can hang your jacket out here if you like."

I thank her and put my jacket on a coat rack near the entrance, wiping my sweaty hands on my pants. Pauline must be the boss; I realize that I never actually got her name when we spoke on the phone.

A large woman, with purpose in her step, comes out a moment later. She gives me a curt smile, shaking my hand with a firm grip.

"Hello, Sophie," she says. "I'm glad you could come in today. We can go talk in my office."

As we pass the front desk, Rachel gives me a little wave. I relax a little; she seems nice. Pauline takes me to a room with a large desk and some chairs. That's about it. No pictures on the walls, not even books on the bookshelves.

"Have a seat," she says, and she sits down on the big office chair on the other side of the desk. "Tell me about yourself."

I tell her about the work I did at the grocery store, only embellishing a little. I tell her that I grew up in town, and everything else I can think of. Except for my social media profile. I don't think she'll be particularly impressed by some suggestive images online.

We talk for another half hour, and she tells me more about what the job entails. It sounds pretty straightforward, and I relax more and more the longer we talk.

"Well, I think this all sounds very good, Sophie," Pauline finishes and places her hands on the desk in front of her. "If you're interested, I would be happy to give you the position."

I nearly jump out of my seat. "Really? Thank you so much. I'm very interested!"

"Good." A small smile tugs on Pauline's lips. "You'll be following a more senior member of the staff for your first week or so, but then you'll be expected to work independently. It can get a little stressful at times, so I hope you can handle that."

I nod eagerly. "Not a problem."

"Great. So, how soon can you start?"

"I can start right away," I tell her, still in awe that I actually got the job.

"Okay, then. How about you get here around seven-thirty tomorrow morning?" Pauline asks. "We'll get you some scrubs, and you can get started with your training."

"Sounds good to me!"

Pauline leaves me there for a moment to get some

paperwork, and I do a little dance in my seat. I'll be making money again. I didn't even ask about the pay, but it can't be worse than what I made at the grocery store.

When she places the contract before me, I see that it is, in fact, almost as bad as the pay at my last job, but I don't care. It's a salary, at least. I don't have a lot of other options, so I sign my name on the dotted line, and Pauline shows me out.

"Welcome to the North Pole Home for Seniors," she congratulates me and shakes my hand. "I'll see you tomorrow morning."

CHAPTER 13

I get to work right on time, and I'm greeted by a woman about my own age named Allie. She shows me where I can find the scrubs that everyone wears, and I get my own locker for my things. I'm not allowed to have my phone on me when I'm working, and it kind of sucks having to leave it in my bag. But I can't exactly do anything about it, so I just leave it there with a smile on my face.

"We'll start with Mrs. Johnson," Allie says as we walk to the first floor. "She's an early riser; most of the others prefer to sleep in."

An old woman is sitting up on her bed, waiting for us, when Allie unlocks the door to her room. Mrs. Johnson was probably a real beauty back in her day, her silvery hair carefully arranged in rollers on top of her head. Her alert eyes meet mine as I step inside.

"Oh," she says. "Who is this?"

"Mrs. Johnson, this is Sophie," Allie introduces me. "It's her first day."

"Hello, Sophie," the old woman says to me. "Welcome to the madhouse."

I smile. I like this woman. "It's nice to meet you, Mrs. Johnson."

"You have nice hair," she says. "That's a good sign; none of these people know how to do my hair."

I look her over. "I don't know," I tell her. "It looks pretty good to me."

Mrs. Johnson scoffs. "You're just saying that because you're new. I'll play along, and we can complain about these people later when we're alone."

Allie gives me a look, and I try to hold back a laugh.

"What would you like to wear today, Mrs. Johnson?" Allie asks. The old woman pauses to think about it, her head tilted to the side.

"I think I'd like my green jumpsuit today. Thank you, Allie. Oh, with my leopard brooch."

Allie shows me to a small closet where beautiful

clothes are hung up neatly on copper hangers. She pulls out a green jumpsuit and hands it to me.

"I'll help Mrs. Johnson out of bed, and when we come back from her shower, you can help her get dressed. Okay? And you can find her leopard brooch in her jewelry box on the dresser."

I nod, grateful that I don't have to help the old woman shower on my first day. I expect Mrs. Johnson to lean heavily on Allie, but as they leave for the bathroom, the woman is walking tall and proud. I wonder how old she is. Probably in her late eighties. She looks pretty good for her age, I have to say.

While they're gone, I admire the luxurious fabric of Mrs. Johnson's clothes. She's obviously a woman who takes great pride in her appearance. I think I'm going to enjoy working with her. I go through the most gorgeous pieces of jewelry I think I've ever seen in my life until I find the right brooch. I wonder what sort of life Mrs. Johnson used to lead with things like these.

They come back after only a few minutes, and Allie gives me an expectant look. I walk over to Mrs. Johnson, and together, we get her into the jumpsuit. I fasten the brooch on her lapel, and she seems pleased with the placement.

"Now, if you would do my hair," she says. "I like it in loose curls."

"Alright," I respond and stand behind her as she sits in front of a mirror on the wall.

I carefully remove the rolls from her long, white

hair, and it cascades down her shoulders. I'm not used to seeing old women with hairstyles like this; most tend to keep their hair short.

Mrs. Johnson hands me a brush and tells me to go through her hair carefully. I brush through the long locks gently, making sure not to disrupt the curls. When I'm done, she reaches for a bobby pin, and with hands that are shaking ever so slightly, she pins her hair away from her face. She looks like a movie star from the forties.

"You look great!" I tell her, and I really mean it. She smiles at me, then turns to Allie.

"I like this one; make sure she sticks around."

I then help her put on some red lipstick, finishing off her look. When we move onto the next resident, I turn to Allie.

"She must be popular with the men around here."

Allie laughs. "You have no idea. They all want to marry her. You'd think they're still in their twenties with the way they're prancing around."

Most of the other residents are a bit more run-down than Mrs. Johnson, but they all welcome me and tell me that they hope I'll like it here. I help some of them get into wheelchairs, and a few want me to read the newspaper to them before it's time for break-fast. Food is served in the dining hall, and I get to meet some more of my new coworkers as we all gather together.

"You get to eat, too," Allie says. "We sit with the residents and keep them company, so Pauline wants us to share a meal with them. Makes it seem a little bit more relaxed, you know?"

I get food? On the job? This is looking better and better by the minute! I'm sitting next to an older man who looks like he's well over a hundred years old. His mind is calm, though, and he seems to enjoy talking. Before the meal is up, I know every name of his grandkids, as well as his great-grandkids.

"My oldest great-granddaughter is expecting," he says. "Can you believe it? I'll be a great-great-grand-father. I'm much too young for that."

"Oh, yes," I agree. "You can't be a day over seventy."

"Ha!" he exclaims, and I jump at the sudden laugh. "A hundred and two. Can you believe it?"

I totally can. "No, I can't."

"The secret is to eat well and exercise," he tells me conspiratorially, as if he's giving me the answer to all the secrets of the universe. "And to make love often."

I choke on my water as I burst out laughing. "I'll keep that in mind."

"Let's not scare Sophie off on her first day, Mr. Wilson," Allie says, amusement in her tone.

"Oh, bah!" he yells with a wave of his hand. "She's a grown woman, isn't she? Lovemaking is a wonderful part of life; nothing to be ashamed of."

"Alright, that's probably enough," she says with a smile. "Would you like some more coffee?"

"Of course, I do. What a silly question."

THE REST of the day goes by in a flurry. I meet so many new people that I'm having a hard time remembering their names. But I'm actually enjoying myself. I wasn't so sure I would. Right before I'm supposed to leave for the day, Pauline finds me and Allie.

"So," she begins, "everything go okay today?"

"I think so," I tell her. *I hope so.*

"She's been great," Allie says. "The residents love her already."

"Oh, I'm so glad!" Pauline cheers and pats me on the shoulder. "I hope you'll like it here, Sophie. I think it's very important that my staff members are happy, so don't hesitate to come to me if there are any issues."

I nod. "I will. Thank you."

I'm over the moon as I head back to my place from the seniors' home, pleasantly surprised at how much I enjoyed myself. I decide to reward myself with some coffee on my way home from work. Not that I don't have to worry about money, but I figure I can afford such a small luxury. I get my latte and am just about to head back outside when I freeze. Tanner is right outside the door!

And he's looking at me.

CHAPTER 14

$\mathcal{I}$ almost consider not going outside, but that's just ridiculous. We both live in this small town; we were bound to run into each other at some point. I take a deep breath, then I put a smile on my face as I step outside.

"Tanner," I say his name, keeping my tone light. "It's good to see you."

"You, too," he says back, and I can smell his cologne with how close we're standing. Ugh, I had almost forgotten how gorgeous he is. "How have you been?" he asks.

"Oh, great! I actually got a new job," I tell him. "First day today."

"Really?" He actually looks happy for me. "What's the job?"

"Caregiver over at the North Pole Home for Seniors," I say. "Maybe not the most glamorous job, but…" I stop myself. Why am I putting down the job I actually really like? "But as you said, things don't always have to be glamorous to be enjoyed."

"Right." He hesitates, and then he continues. "You want to talk for a bit? I'd love to catch up."

I probably shouldn't. "Okay, sure."

"Just let me get a coffee, and we can take a walk or something."

My heart is racing when he goes into the coffee shop. I can't believe I've run into him like this. He looks so good, and I hope I don't look too rough after my day at the seniors' home. Not that it matters, anyway; we're not together anymore. I can look as rough as I want.

He comes back outside after just a few minutes, and we start walking down the street. There are people everywhere, mostly tourists who have come to the North Pole for the holiday. There's Christmas music coming from the different shops, and the ground is covered with snow. It's beautiful, I have to admit.

Tanner glances over at me, and our eyes meet for a second. He smiles as I look away again.

"So," Tanner says, "I've seen you online."

I raised an eyebrow. "Really?"

"Yeah, I saw some of your pictures."

I want to ask if he likes them, but I don't know what he thinks of the kind of pictures I'm posting. "Well, you inspired me," I reply.

"Do you enjoy it?" he asks, and I nod.

"I do, actually. It's a lot of fun. You were right; it's pretty rewarding when people engage with your content."

"I was just a little surprised at the type of content you put up. There's nothing wrong with it; there really isn't. At least, not if that's what you want to do."

I scowl at him. "But…?"

"It just seems so different from the person I got to know before," he says. "I just want to make sure you know what you're doing."

I don't know what to say. "You didn't like the person I was before." I don't mean to say it, but the words just slipped out. Tanner stops walking, taking my arm to stop me, too.

"Sophie, you know that's not true. I did like you. I liked you a lot. We just wanted—"

"Different things, I know." I want to sink into a hole in the ground. "Why do you care what I post? I'm an adult, Tanner. I don't need you looking out for me."

"I know. I just want to make sure you're alright." He looks like he actually means it. The jerk!

"Well, I'm fine," I retort and pull my hand away from him. "I'm getting bigger and bigger every day. People actually like what I put out there."

Tanner sighs. "Right. But what kind of people are enjoying what you put out there?"

"There's nothing wrong with being a little sexy. I'm a very sexual person, and I can't help if people like that. Besides, it's not like I'm doing porn or anything."

"Okay." Tanner nods. "As long as you know what you're doing."

"I do." There's no missing the finality in my tone. "Thanks for your concern, but I'm good. Besides, I've got a collab with Patrick Amaranth coming up, so I'd say things are going pretty well."

"Patrick Amaranth?" Tanner asks. "Are you serious?"

"Why wouldn't I be?" I ask back, sounding a bit more defensive than I mean to. "It's been in the works for a while; we're just waiting for the right time."

"Are we talking about the same Patrick Amaranth?" he asks, his voice dripping with skepticism. "The tech guy?"

"Yeah," I respond with confidence, starting to get a little exasperated with his doubt. The fact that I haven't actually made any such deal with Patrick is another story. "Is that so hard to believe?"

Tanner opens his mouth, only to close it again. He

seems to be choosing his next words carefully. "It's just that… You guys don't exactly have overlapping audiences. But that's great. I'm happy for you."

"You don't sound like you're happy for me."

Tanner sighs, and for a moment, I think he's going to touch me. Take my hand or caress my face or something. But he doesn't. Why does that make me feel so disappointed?

"Sophie, I didn't mean to upset you."

"You didn't upset me, promise," I bluff, and then I force a smile. I want to go home. I want to not be there next to him, pretending we're friends. A lump forms in my throat, and I swallow it down. "It was nice seeing you again, Tanner. Take care of yourself."

I turn around and start walking quickly down the street. I don't want him to follow me, but at the same time, that's *all* I want. Why did I have to run into him today? I was having such a good day, and now I just feel kind of shitty. I need to turn things up a notch. I *really* need to secure this thing with Patrick, too.

And I need more followers. No more buying them in the thousands, or even the five thousands. I will have to go for the next level up. I have a job now; it should be fine.

I grab my laptop as soon as I arrive back home, and I buy ten thousand new followers. I'll keep it up until I'm on Tanner's level; I just have to space it out a little. When I check my bank account, there's just enough there to cover my upcoming electricity bill. *Shit.*

I try not to panic. I'll get paid by the end of the week. I just can't buy anything else until then. If I run out of gas, I'll just walk to work. I could use the exercise. And it's not like this is something I'm going to do forever, just until I'm bigger than Tanner. A few more months, and then I can stop and start saving up again.

I spend the rest of the evening pitching to more companies for sponsorships. So far, I don't have anyone who's interested, and I don't understand why. I have thousands of followers. Thousands! They should be coming to me, begging me to promote their products. I've even mentioned the potential of having Patrick Amaranth onboard, but I guess they must think I'm lying.

I post a picture of myself on my bed, the shot just showing my legs against the mattress. A few likes come through, but not much more than that. I pull up my conversation with Patrick and read through our messages. I can't afford to take things slow anymore. I need this to work.

I need it to work *now*.

CHAPTER 15

It's late, and I have work in the morning, but I can't get my mind to shut up. So, I write to Patrick, giving this one more try. After some pleasantries, I cut right to the chase.

Look, you've been following me for a while and are obviously liking what I put out there. Would it really be so bad if we were to collaborate on something? Do you have any idea how much something like that would do for me?

I kind of wish I could take the message back as

soon as I sent it, but it's too late. Patrick is already typing out a response.

You understand I get requests like this all the time, right? Don't get me wrong, I like talking to you. I like your pictures, too. But I can't just sell out my brand like that. I've worked hard to build that. I won't compromise my professional integrity just because some hot girl asks me to shout her out. It doesn't work like that. Besides, what's in it for me?

What do you want?

I wait for him to type, hoping he won't get creepy on me. Then his message pops up on my screen.

Honestly, there's nothing you have that would make me do this. Sorry, Sophie.

Patrick, I really need this.

Why? Is clout really that important to you?

I type without thinking. *I need to get more followers than this guy I used to date. That's all I want. Just give me a shout-out, and I can be done.*

Damn it. I shouldn't have said that. It looks pathetic, even to me, as I read through my words again.

That's why you're doing this? Are you serious? Sophie, I say this with love. Get help.

His words hit me like a punch to the gut. I put down my phone, and to my annoyance, it feels like I might start crying. What for? I took a risk, and it didn't pay off. But I know that's not it. For the first time since starting all this, I feel ashamed.

I don't fall asleep for hours.

I START to get the hang of things at work pretty quickly over the next few days. Allie lets me do quite a lot by myself, and I only have to ask her for directions every once in a while. I like working with the old people. They're fun, and they have a lot of stories to tell. I know the other members of the staff have heard their stories a thousand times before, but I think they like telling them to me. A fresh pair of ears.

I mostly enjoy working with Mrs. Johnson; she's funny. She seems more like a friend than someone I'm taking care of. It feels good to keep busy, and when I get home, I'm too exhausted to think about anything else.

But then Mrs. Johnson brings up a topic I'd rather not talk about during our little morning routine together.

"Do you have a boyfriend, dear?" she asks one day as I'm fixing her hair in her usual style.

I shake my head. "I don't. Not anymore."

"No? Did he break your heart?"

"We weren't together long enough for him to break my heart," I explain and put down the brush.

"That's not true. I can see it in your eyes," she says and pins her hair back. I grab her red lipstick and swivel her chair around so I can put it on.

"We were only together for a few weeks; it wasn't that serious."

"What happened? If you don't mind me asking."

I laugh. "As if you care if I mind or not." I pause. "I came on a little strong, I think. Maybe I was too clingy. He said he liked me, but we wanted different things. We're moving at different speeds." I leave out all the other stuff. I'm not sure I want to know her thoughts about what I have been up to online over the past few weeks.

Mrs. Johnson seems to consider what I said. "Well, did you?" she asks. "Come on too strong?"

I'm surprised at her question, butting into my private life like that. "I don't know. Maybe. I just really liked him. I wanted to talk to him all the time.

"Well, that's all well and good, dear. But sometimes, we can suffocate the people we care about if we don't give them space. Within reason, of course. You shouldn't be scared to show someone that you care about them."

"Yeah, I guess. It's too late now, anyway," I tell her as I'm finishing her makeup.

"Why is that?"

I frown at her. "Isn't it obvious? He thought I was too annoying. I told you."

"No, you didn't tell me that," she protests. "You told me that he liked you, but that you moved at different speeds. That sort of thing can be remedied. Have you seen him since the breakup?"

"We had coffee a little while back."

"That's good. What did you talk about?"

I can't possibly tell her about the pictures I post online; she wouldn't understand. "He was just worried about me. About some choices I've made. But that's none of his business, anyway."

"It seems like you hold a lot of resentment toward him," Mrs. Johnson speculates. "Why is that?"

"Well, he broke up with me. Of course, I'm resentful."

"But it sounds like he cares about you, still. That's a good foundation to build on. You obviously still care about him, deep down."

"I just want to show him that I'm just as good as him," I say without really meaning to.

"Of course, you're as good as him. Why wouldn't you be? But if you want any chance of the two of you getting back together, maybe it's time to let go of some of that resentment. If you think you can."

"Who said I want to get back together with him?"

"It's written all over your face, dear Sophie," Mrs. Johnson says with a teasing grin. "Don't think you can trick me. I've lived a long time. I know when people are fooling themselves."

"Can we talk about something else, please?"

She grins even wider, but she lets me move on. We talk a little bit about everything and nothing until I have to move on to the next resident. Mrs. Johnson's words echo through my brain as I go about my work. Maybe I *have* been resentful. I've acted crazy with this whole situation, that's for sure. I'm not sure if I would want to get back together with Tanner. I just know that I can't keep going like this anymore. I have to let him and my stupid follower stunt go. Or I have to fight for what I want.

I have to fight for *who* I want.

———

THAT FRIDAY, Allie comes up to me after our shift.

"Hey, do you want to grab a drink or something tonight? Might be fun to hang out outside of work for once."

I was planning on just having a quiet night in, but it actually sounds kind of fun to go out with her instead. "Okay," I agree. "I'd like that."

"Let's meet up by the bar later then. I just want to go home and take a shower first."

"Sure. I'll meet you around eight?"

Allie nods. "Sounds good."

I pull on a new pair of jeans and a pretty light-green top that sits nicely on my body. I leave my hair wavy and do a subtle cat eye with plenty of mascara. It's simple, but I feel pretty. I feel strong. I decide to walk down to the bar where we are meeting up, leaving my car at home. I need the fresh air.

Allie is already waiting outside the bar, her blond hair up in a high ponytail. She looks really good in her floral shirt and tight jeans, and she waves at me as I come closer with a big smile on her face.

"This is going to be so much fun!" she cheers and pulls me in for a hug. "I haven't been out in ages."

"Me, neither," I admit, and I realize that I can't

even remember the last time I went out with a girlfriend.

The bar is pretty packed since it's one of the few places where you can go out in this town, but we manage to find a table. We get our drinks and sit down.

"Any cute guys here tonight?" she asks, a twinkle in her eye. Oh, so someone's on the prowl.

"Why?" I ask and grin at her. "Are you looking to take someone home tonight?"

She laughs. "Maybe. Would that be so bad?"

I shake my head. "Not at all. Go for it! I can be your wingman."

"I don't know," she then whispers. "Not a lot of promising subjects so far."

I know what she means. Most of the guys in here are at least twenty years older than us, and not in a sexy silver fox kind of way. After a while, however, Allie locks eyes with a guy across the bar.

"What do you think about him?" she asks me, and I look over. It's a guy in his early thirties, and he's making eyes at her in an extremely obvious way. He's wearing a flannel shirt and has a baseball cap on backwards. Not exactly my type, but I guess he's kind of cute.

"Sure, go for it."

Allie knocks back her drink. "I feel like I'm abandoning you," she says, and I scoff at her.

"Please, go get laid. You worked hard this week; you deserve some stress relief."

She grins at me, and then she gets up from her chair. "How do I look?"

"You look hot. Go get him."

I watch as she goes up to the guy, shaking his hand. He looks at her as if she's the prettiest thing he has ever seen, laughing at something she said. They walk to the bar together, and he buys her a drink. I sip my own cocktail, smiling wide as her eyes find mine, and she gives me a big thumbs up. I take it that things are going well.

I look around the bar at the people there and realize that I only recognize about half the faces. Probably a lot of tourists here tonight. But there are some familiar faces, too, even some people I went to high school with. Oh, the joys of living in a small town.

"Hi, there." A man in his forties suddenly comes up to me, standing behind Allie's empty chair. I look at him with a smile.

"Hi."

"Look, would you mind taking a picture?"

I'm stunned. Has this guy recognized me from my profile online? I know I decided not to keep up with all that, but a small part of me still gets excited at the prospect of getting recognized.

"Sure," I say, smiling sweetly at him. "No problem. Happy to."

This is unreal, having someone who wants to take a picture with me. He hands me his phone and waves his friend over.

"We want to get a picture with the big buck head in the background," he says and points to the stuffed buck that's mounted on the wall behind him. "Is that okay?"

I nod. "Okay, sure. Let's do it."

The man throws an arm around his friend's shoulders, and they smile wide for the camera. I slide up beside them and angle the camera so that I get us all in the frame. The guy chuckles.

"Wait, what are you doing?" he asks.

"Taking the picture," I tell him. *Is he being serious?*

"Yeah, but just with my friend and me. No offense, but I don't know you. I don't want you in the picture. Sorry."

I feel my cheeks burning. He doesn't want a picture of me; he just wants me to take one of him and his friend. He hasn't recognized me after all. I'm just the first loser he saw who looked like she didn't have a life. Just another sign that I need to stop with this whole charade. I can't believe I'm stupid enough to think he wanted to take a picture with me!

"Of course," I say quickly. "Sorry, I just thought…"

I see him and his friend exchange a look. I must seem so weird. I snap the picture of them and hand the man his phone back. He thanks me, his eyes lingering on my chest.

"Thanks," he says. "Listen, maybe my friend and I here can buy you a drink. As a thank you for your photography services."

It's probably supposed to be a joke, but I don't laugh. "I'm good, thanks."

"Oh, come on," he insists. "You look pretty lonely; we'll show you a good time."

I'm just about to tell him no again when a familiar voice speaks up.

"She said no."

I turn around and find myself face-to-face with Tanner.

CHAPTER 16

"Hey, man. Take it easy!" the man shouts. "Is she your girlfriend or something?"

"Sophie, do you want to leave?" Tanner asks, ignoring the man. I nod. I *do* want to leave.

"Just let me tell my friend," I say quietly. Allie practically has the guy eating out of the palm of her hand when I find them. He's hanging onto every word she says, and when I come over and interrupt their conversation, it looks like he has woken up from a daze.

"I'm gonna go," I say to her. "Are you okay to stay?"

Allie nods. "Of course." She looks to my side, where Tanner has sidled up to me. "Um, hi, there."

"Hello," Tanner says, sounding more serious than he usually does.

"Yeah, so I'm going," I repeat to Allie, not in the mood to explain who Tanner is and why I'm leaving with him. Allie is giving me a look. No doubt I will have to tell her everything on Monday.

"Okay, have fun!" she exclaims, and I smile at her. "You, too."

We walk away in silence, Tanner's body right next to mine all the way out. I put on my coat, and my breath makes a cloud in front of me when I step outside. It's really cold, and I rub my hands together.

"Don't you have any gloves?" Tanner asks.

I shake my head. "I forgot them at home."

"Here," he says, and before I can register it, he's holding both my hands in his. He's deliciously warm, and I relax a little. "Better?"

"Yeah. Better."

We just stand there for a moment, and it should probably feel strange. It doesn't, though.

"What was up with those guys?" he asks.

I just shrug. "They were just being obnoxious. Thanks for sticking up for me."

"I didn't like the way they were looking at you."

I smile. "Why do you care if someone's looking at me?"

He doesn't say anything. Just presses his lips together and looks down at me. "You haven't posted in a while," he says.

"Are you keeping tabs on me or something?" I ask. "I've just been busy. I've been working a lot."

"That girl in there," he says and nods over to the bar, "do you guys work together?"

"We do. Why?"

He shrugs. "It's just nice to see that you've made some friends. You seem to really like your job."

"I do, actually," I admit. "It's a lot more fun than I thought it would be."

Tanner rubs my cold hands some more. He doesn't look as angry now. I guess he's calmed down out here in the cold. "I'm glad. So, you're down with the oldies now, huh?"

I burst out laughing. "Down with the oldies?"

He grins. "Yes. Do you like them?"

"They're great," I tell him. "We're totally down. Dawg!"

"Has any of the men proposed to you yet?" he asks, an amused twinkle in his eyes.

"No, I'm not their type. They're all lusting after Mrs. Johnson."

"Is she pretty?"

"So pretty. Looks like a silent film actress."

"Maybe I'll have to come with you to work one day," he says. "I want to meet this woman."

I scoff. "I don't think so. She already gets enough male attention. I bet she wouldn't mind meeting *you*, though."

Tanner raises an eyebrow. "Yeah? Why is that? Have you told her about me?"

I feel myself blush. "Maybe."

"Good things, I hope."

I look up at him, my smile falling slightly. "Why are you being all… I don't know. Charming."

"You say that like it's a bad thing."

I pull my hands away. "It's confusing."

His expression turns serious. "Sorry. It's just so nice to see you again."

"What do you want me to say to that?" I ask him. Tanner bites his lip, regarding me.

"You don't need to say anything if you don't want to. That's not why I said it." He's quiet for a moment. "Are you still mad at me?"

I sigh. "I was never mad at you, Tanner. Not really. I just… you kind of made me feel like crap."

"I know. I do feel bad about that." Tanner steps closer and tucks a strand of hair behind my ear. "You know, I've been thinking. Maybe I was…"

"Sophie!"

Lacey from the grocery store is waving at me, obviously drunk. She's holding onto a guy whom I recognize as her husband, and he looks equally out of it. I force a smile as she comes over to me, engulfing me in a tight hug.

"It's so good to see you!" she practically screams,

slurring her words a bit. "It's been so boring at work without you."

"It's good to see you, Lacey," I say back, willing her to go away. Her timing couldn't have been worse; I want to know what Tanner was about to say.

"You know, the girl who replaced you is such a little know-it-all. She thinks she's better than everyone. I swear, one day, I'll…"

I let her go on her little spiel. Tanner is watching me, and I can't help but watch him back. What was he about to say? I search his face, but he's impossible to read.

"So, how's the new job?" Lacey asks. "I could never do that, wiping old peoples' butts."

I don't have the energy to tell her that I don't actually do that, so I just smile and tell her that it's great. Lacey goes on another spiel, and I look over at Tanner again. He mouths something to me as Lacey's voice keeps going and going.

I'll call you later.

I nod, and there's a flutter in my stomach. Tanner gives me a small smile before he walks away. My eyes are set on his back until he rounds a corner and is out of sight.

"Lacey, it was really nice seeing you again," I say after a while, interrupting her. "I actually have to get home."

"Oh, okay," she stutters and pulls me in for another hug. "I'll see you around, Sophie."

Lacey and her husband stagger back inside the

bar, and I stand there for a moment. I don't want to go home to my empty apartment. It would be so easy to just go back inside and drag some guy along back to my place, but I don't want that, either. The only guy I want to take home with me just walked away.

I pull out my phone, and my finger hovers over Tanner's name in my contact list. I want to talk to him; I want to *really* talk. And I want to figure myself out. Figure out why I felt the need to beat him with the whole social media thing. Even as the thought enters my brain, I'm struck by how ridiculous it sounds.

What has this all accomplished, anyway? I bet Tanner doesn't even notice how many followers I have. Now that I think about it, I don't see a reason why he would. For a while, I loved getting comments from guys on my feed. I loved reading their words about my body. It was addictive. It was nice to feel desired. But now… I don't know. I'm still alone. No matter how many DMs I get.

And I'm broke. Even with my salary, I am still paying late fees on everything I bought over the past few weeks. I couldn't keep up in the end. It's going to take a while before I pay it all off. What a waste.

I get home and throw myself onto the bed, not bothering to take my makeup off. Suddenly, exhaustion crashes into me, and I just want to sleep. I kick off my shoes and crawl under the covers. I'll deal with reality tomorrow.

CHAPTER 17

My phone rings early the next morning. I sit up in bed, trying to locate it. I find it underneath one of my pillows, and when I see Tanner's name pop up, my heart starts racing. I take a deep breath, and then I answer.

"Hello?"

"Sophie," he says. "I'm sorry if I woke you up. I just couldn't wait any longer to talk to you."

I clear my throat and drag a hand through my

hair. "It's okay," I reply, trying to sound calm. "You wanted to speak to me about something?"

"Yes, if you'd be okay with that." He sounds a little nervous. "Can I come over?"

I look around me. The place is a mess. *I'm* a mess. "Give me an hour."

I chug some water and take a quick shower. Then I run around and pick up around the apartment, shoving things into drawers and closets to get them out of sight. My heart is racing when there's a knock on the door. Okay, I can do this.

Tanner is looking obnoxiously good in his suede jacket and the fedora on his head. "Hi," he says, and for a moment, I think he's going to kiss me. But he just leans in for a hug, holding me close. I wrap my arms around his waist, allowing myself to breathe him in. I don't think I've realized just how much I've missed him.

"Come in," I tell him as we pull apart. He follows me inside, and when I offer him some coffee, he takes the mug right away.

"You remembered how I take it," he says.

I smile. "It's not very complicated. A splash of milk is not that hard to remember."

"Still," he repeats. I melt under his gaze. "You remembered."

We sit down on the couch, and neither of us say anything. My mind is completely blank, and Tanner seems to be on the verge of speaking, only to change his mind again. After several minutes of this, I can't take it anymore.

"What did you want to talk to me about?"

He clears his throat and puts the mug on the coffee table. "I want to talk about what happened between us."

"What's there to talk about?" I ask, scared that he's going to rip open those wounds again. "We were just not on the same page, and that's all there is to it."

"But I feel like I acted too quickly," Tanner says. "I was kind of a jerk to you."

"But you were right. I *did* come on too strong. I can see that now. Even though that wasn't my intention. I just wanted to talk to you."

"I know. I guess I kind of got scared."

"Scared? How?"

Tanner takes my hand, stroking his thumb over my knuckles. "I liked you so much. I haven't felt like that since my ex, and…"

"And she cheated on you. I wouldn't do that, though."

"No, I know. I just figured we would crash and burn some other way, and I was so stressed at that conference. When you kept calling, I just sort of snapped. I convinced myself that we weren't right for each other, that we moved at different speeds. But that's bullshit."

I huff out a laugh. "Kind of is, yeah."

"Then when I saw you online, I figured I had made the right decision," Tanner continued. "I didn't recognize the person I saw on your profile. It didn't seem like you."

I nod. "Okay, I can see that. It wasn't me. At least, not entirely. But I did have fun, at least at the beginning. I got too hung up on the whole thing in the end, though. I let it take over my life."

"It happens," he says. "It's addicting, getting all that attention. Stuff like that doesn't matter, however. I know it's my job, but I don't care about the numbers. You shouldn't either."

"No, I guess I shouldn't."

He moves closer to me on the couch. "I haven't been able to stop thinking about you, Sophie. I made a mistake."

My heart stops. "What are you saying?"

"I'm saying that I want to try this again. I want you, Sophie. I want you so bad."

I stare at him. Am I really hearing this right? "You want me?"

"I've wanted you all along. I'm really sorry for how I ended things. It was not what I want; I know that now."

My head is spinning. I've spent months trying to beat Tanner, missing him like crazy in the meantime. And now he's saying that he wants me back?

"I understand if I'm too late," he continues. "I don't expect you to still feel the same way about me."

I think back on the past few weeks. On the bots, on all the time and money I've wasted. It was all fake.

He is real.

I lean in, closing the gap between us. Kissing him feels like coming home after a long trip. Safe. He's cupping my face, kissing me back, then opening up when I trace my tongue along the edge of his lips. I press myself against him until I straddle his lap on the couch. Tanner smiles against my lips.

"Does this mean I'm forgiven?"

"We'll see," I tease. "It depends."

"On what?"

I kiss his neck and bite down gently on the sensitive skin there. "It depends on how good this next part is."

He laughs. "Oh, really? Well, I better make it good then."

I nod. "You better."

He pulls me down for another kiss. There's a new sense of urgency that wasn't there before, and I feel his arousal underneath my body. My heart is pounding against his chest, and it wouldn't surprise me if he can feel my every heartbeat.

His hands slide in under my shirt, and I raise my arms as he takes it off of me. *Finally*. Finally, his hands are on me, touching me with such *want* and *need* that I don't know what to do with myself.

Tanner grabs hold of me, and I gasp as he flips me onto my back. His pupils are so enlarged that I can almost not see the color around them, and he's breathing heavily. He's pressing kisses to my cheek, my jaw, my neck. One piece of clothing after another makes its way to the floor, until I'm naked under his gaze. Tanner's shirt is on the floor as well, and the rest of his clothes soon follow. I want to tell him to go find a condom, but I lose all ability to form coherent sentences when he takes one breast into his mouth, swirling his tongue around my nipple.

"How's it looking so far?" he asks with a grin. "Am I forgiven yet?"

I pretend to think it over, biting my bottom lip. "The jury is still out on that."

He kisses my stomach, and a low chuckle escapes him. "Really? I better keep going then."

He hooks his arms underneath my legs and pulls me down to his face. I cry out as he puts his mouth on me, lapping at my most sensitive part. He's going slow, and he drives me crazy with the languid movements of his tongue, and the way he peers up at me through hooded eyes. God, he's so beautiful. He keeps a steady rhythm, and when he increases the pace ever so slightly, I almost fall off the couch.

"Good?" he asks, and I can tell he's trying not to laugh.

"Don't look so smug," I tell him, but I can't wipe the pleased grin off my face. "Keep going."

"Yes, ma'am."

He's going faster now, and I weave my fingers into his hair, needing to feel him as he brings me closer and closer to the edge. With one final stroke of his tongue, release shoots through me, making me writhe in his grip. Tanner holds me in place, not letting up with his tongue. A second orgasm quickly follows the first, and I just keep calling out his name as waves of pleasure roll through me.

"Am I forgiven yet?"

I laugh; I can't help myself. "I'd say so." I glance down at him, and the heat in his eyes sends another jolt of arousal through me.

"I want you, Tanner. Right now."

"Thank God for that," he praises, making his way up my body. He kisses me long and deep, and I feel his hard length press against my entrance. "Let me get a condom, okay?"

I nod, about to tell him where I keep them when he reaches for his pants and pulls out his wallet. He has a packet in there, and he tears it open. He's back on top of me in no time, and I part my legs for him. He moans as he aligns himself with me and slowly pushes in.

"I've dreamt about this for so long," he whispers into my ear, capturing my lips into another kiss. I want to say that I have, too, but then he's moving, and all I can think about is the way he feels inside of me. How full I feel, how good his every thrust feels.

He's looking down into my eyes, and at that moment, I'm so happy I could burst. I reach up and touch his cheek, and he leans into my touch. Kisses my wrist, and then he moves faster. Our eyes lock once again as he falls over the edge, the most delicious sounds coming from his lips. I follow soon after; the sight of him so completely undone is just about the hottest thing I've ever seen.

He keeps kissing me, little sweet pecks on the lips that make me laugh in the afterglow of what we just did. Tanner is laughing, too, and he just keeps touching me; it's like he can't help himself either. Not that I mind.

Not one bit.

CHAPTER 18

"Someone's happy today."

I pull out Mrs. Johnson's clothes from her closet. She has chosen a purple jumpsuit today, and I smile at her. I can't seem to stop. "What's not to be happy about?"

She shakes her head at me. "No, no, don't give me that. Something happened, and I want to know about it."

"Nosy," I tell her and help her into her clothes. "Fine. Do you remember the man we talked about?"

"The one who broke your heart? Yes, of course."

"He didn't break my heart, exactly," I protest, even though he kind of did. "Well, we've talked things out."

"Oh, you've talked things out, have you?" She raises an eyebrow and gives me a knowing smirk. "I wasn't born yesterday, dear Sophie. I know what a smile like that means. Is his member very large?"

I almost choke on my saliva. "Mrs. Johnson!"

"Oh, we're all adults here. Let me live vicariously through your escapades. Tell me more."

"I'm not telling you about his… well, *that*."

"Very well," she says and sits down in front of the mirror. "If you won't tell me the fun bits, then at least tell me what was said between the two of you."

I think for a moment. I haven't really thought through what happened myself. Might be nice to talk it out with Mrs. Johnson. "He told me that he'd made a mistake. That he's wanted to be with me all along."

"What stopped him from coming to you earlier? Seems silly to me."

I consider telling her about my profile. "I have this social media profile. Do you know what that is?"

"Of course, don't be rude. I'm well aware of such things."

"Okay, good. I posted some pictures of myself on there, and he saw them. He thought I had changed into someone I'm not."

"Are they lewd pictures?"

"Well," I hesitate for a second, "they're not lewd, exactly. Just… suggestive. Yes. Let's go with suggestive."

"How exciting!" She claps her hands together. "And he had a problem with that?"

"Not a problem. He just didn't think it was like me. He thought I had become someone else."

"And so, what if you had? We all change throughout the course of our life. That is a good thing."

I consider her words. I suppose she's right, but I didn't really post those pictures for the right reasons. I knew they would do well, so I kept going. I enjoyed posting on my page, but I was just as excited about that first photo of me on my couch. The one where I set up all the fairy lights and really created something. I liked the process of it, the creativity. And while it was fun getting validation from strangers for a while, I'm very much over it by now. I don't want to keep posting the way I've been doing. I want to change direction. Go back to what I actually find fun.

When I go on my break, I pull my phone out of my locker. There's no one else in the staff room, so I pull up my profile. I see the number that tells me the number of followers I have. How many of those are even real? Out of the tens of thousands, maybe only a couple hundred are actual people.

I scroll through my pictures, reading the comments underneath them. I see DonnieWylde93, and a bit later, I see Sam's name, too. When I go through my DMs, I just open a few before I delete them all. I don't want to read what all these strangers have to say about me.

I go back to my profile, and I am struck with a thought. I should just delete it all. The whole page. Can I really do that? For a second, all the money I've spent on this account stops me. But then I shake my head. I can't get that money back anyway. But I can move forward from this strange period of my life.

I go to my settings and find the *delete account* option at the very bottom, the letters standing out to me in red. I swallow, hovering with my thumb over it for several minutes.

I only have five minutes left on my break when I finally decide to do it. I press *delete account*, and then I confirm that I actually want to do it. It takes a few seconds, and then it's all gone. Just like that.

I let out a breath. That wasn't so bad. It was actually pretty liberating. I will probably create a different account later, but it's only going to be for fun. I don't need all that anymore. The followers, the likes, the comments. I have a job I love, and I've made a friend in Allie. I have Tanner. For the first time in a long time, maybe ever, it feels like I have direction in my life. Like I have purpose. Things are good.

Things are really, really good.

I wake up to a soft kiss on my lips. Tanner is smiling at me, and he's wearing a Santa hat. *Only* a Santa hat. I prop myself up on my elbows and look at him, laughing.

"Why the hell are you wearing that?"

"To get in the holiday spirit!" he sings. "It's Christmas morning!"

Oh, that's right. I haven't really thought about Christmas much this year. Too much else has been going on. I also need to remember to call my mother later. Tanner pulls me down for another kiss.

"Merry Christmas."

I smile against his lips. "Merry Christmas."

"I made you breakfast," he tells me. I look him up and down.

"Naked?"

"I wore an apron, obviously. It was all very sexy. Too bad you missed it."

"I bet it was." I sit up fully and stretch with a yawn. "Let's have some breakfast then."

"Wait here," he says and springs out of bed. His bare butt goes really well with the hat, I must say. Tanner returns a moment later, carrying a tray of toast and some coffee, and there are some gingerbread cookies on the side. "There you go!" he cheers and places the tray on my lap. "There's cinnamon in the coffee."

"You're so sweet," I whisper to him as I'm nibbling on one of the gingerbread cookies. "Aren't you eating?"

"I'll steal some of your toast."

I snag the tray from him. "Oh, no you don't. This is *my* food."

He laughs. "Of course, how silly of me. Sophie Leigh doesn't share food."

"You can have one of the gingerbread cookies." I offer, and he takes it from me.

"How generous of you."

We spend the entire morning in bed, just lounging and kissing and talking. I'd be content with spending the entire day there, but Tanner tells me it's time to get up far too soon. He drags me into the bathroom for a shower and washes every inch of my body, taking great care to lather every part of me.

After that, he tells me to get dressed in something nice, and I pick out a red, flowy dress that I had just bought. I fix my hair in a fishtail braid that comes down over my left shoulder, and I finish the look with some red lipstick, courtesy of Mrs. Johnson. When I go back out into the living room, Tanner is wearing a crisp dress shirt, with the sleeves rolled up to his elbows, and a pair of slacks that makes him look amazing. He smiles as I join him, pulling me close.

"You're beautiful," he says quietly.

"You don't look too bad yourself," I say back, running a hand up one of his strong arms. "What are we doing?"

"We're having Christmas lunch," he tells me.

"With who?"

"Some friends of yours."

Some friends of mine? My mind goes to Allie, but I know she's working today. Who else is there? Tanner refuses to say, and when he leads me to his car, he makes me put on a blindfold.

"Are you serious?" I ask as he's making sure I can't see anything.

"Dead serious. Don't peek, okay?"

I sigh. "Fine."

He starts up the engine, and I can feel us begin to move. I try to figure out where we're going, but I suspect that Tanner is taking a few extra laps around town just to confuse me. After a while, we pull to a stop, and I reach for the blindfold, eager to get it off me.

"Not yet!" He quickly turns to me and takes my hands away from the knot on the back. "I'll lead you there."

"I really hate surprises, you know that?"

I can practically hear him smile. "I think you'll like this one."

We're walking across some asphalt, my heels clicking all the way until we reach some stairs. Tanner tells me that there are five steps and to be careful. I hold onto his arm and manage to keep upright somehow. I would have worn flats if I'd known I would be climbing stairs completely blind. It gets instantly warmer when we go inside, and I sniff the air. Something smells familiar. There's the scent of food somewhere, but that's not what has caught my attention. There's a smell of disinfectant and heavy perfume mixed into one. I gasp.

"We're at my job!"

Tanner groans. "I told you not to peek."

"I didn't," I assure him. "I can smell it."

"Oh." The blindfold falls away from my eyes. "I guess we don't need this anymore."

I look around. The place is decked out for Christmas. They must have done this today because it wasn't like this when I left work yesterday.

It looks pretty great, actually. Garlands are hanging from the wooden staircase, and there are candles and glitter everywhere. I see a familiar face walking toward us down the hall. Mrs. Johnson is striding down the hallway, dressed in a red jumpsuit, her back straight and her head held high.

"Merry Christmas, Mrs. Johnson," I greet her when she's within earshot.

"The same to you, dear Sophie," she says and squeezes my hands. "And to you, of course, young man."

"Mrs. Johnson, this is Tanner," I introduce him, and the two smile at each other.

"Yes, I figured as much. We spoke on the phone the other day."

I frown. "You did? Why?"

"To set this all up, of course."

I look up at Tanner. "We're celebrating Christmas here?"

He nods. "Is that okay?"

"Okay?" I squeal. "It's perfect!" I fling myself around his neck, pulling him in for a back-breaking hug. I kiss him next, and I don't stop until I hear Mrs. Johnson clear her throat.

"Shall we go into the dining room?" she asks and gestures for us to follow her with an elegant wave of her hand. If I didn't know any better, I'd think she's a mistress of some grand mansion. Maybe she was at some point; she still hasn't told me much about her life.

The dining room is full of residents and members of the staff, and Allie runs over to me as soon as she sees me.

"Merry Christmas!" she squeals. "Isn't this great?"

"It's amazing!" I squeal back. "Who organized all this?"

"We all did," she tells me. "With some help from Tanner here."

I look up at him, and he's blushing a little. "I can't believe you want to spend Christmas here."

"Of course, I do. These are your friends," he says, putting an arm around my waist. "And I would go wherever you go, Sophie. I hope you know that."

I swallow the lump in my throat. This is the best Christmas gift I've ever gotten.

Allie hurries back to the table, and I see a strange face among all the others. But then I remember where I know him from. It's the guy from the bar. I didn't even know Allie had kept seeing him. I need to ask her about it later. He's looking at her like she'd just hung the moon, such adoration in his eyes that I almost start crying. I'm so happy for her.

Hell, I'm so happy for *me*.

Tanner and I sit down close to Allie and her friend, and he introduces himself to us as Brian. Mrs. Johnson is sitting right across from me, and she looks so regal that I can't stop looking at her.

"Didn't your mother teach you that it is rude to stare, Sophie?" she asks sternly and puts a napkin on her lap.

"Nope!" I happily respond and grin at her. "So, I'll just keep staring, thank you very much."

Mrs. Johnson turns to Tanner. "The gall of this girl; can you believe it?"

He smiles and puts an arm over my shoulders. "I know. No manners at all."

"You'll have your hands full with this one," the old woman says. "But something tells me that you don't mind."

I look up at him, and he looks right back. "No," he whispers as he plants a kiss on my cheek, "I don't mind at all."

I lean onto his side, looking out at everyone around us. They all look so happy, and I spot Rachel waving at me from the other end of the table. Then she starts laughing at something a resident says to her, her whole body jiggling in her pretty green blouse. Mrs. Johnson is speaking to Tanner, telling him about how she ended up in town. I just sit back and relax,

Tanner's arm around me. I feel so safe, surrounded by all these people.

I feel so at home.

Tanner glances down at me, smiling at me. I pull him down, kissing him slowly and softly, the happy buzzing of voices surrounding us.

"Are you happy?" he asks, his voice so low that only I can hear him. I nod.

"Yeah. I really, really am."

KATHRYN REIGN

www.ingramcontent.com/pod-product-compliance
Lightning Source LLC
Chambersburg PA
CBHW031025190726
48286CB00003BA/1025